STOP OLLINGER!

When the town of Mud Wagon Creek is destroyed by desperadoes, it is just the start of a twisted trail of revenge for outlaw-boss Bass Ollinger. He has sworn to make society pay for the time he spent in the Oregon State Penitentiary, and he intends to blaze a trail of death and destruction clear from Texas to the Beaver State . . . Riding the border country, Brant Forrest unwittingly rides into Ollinger's path, and comes to the inevitable conclusion: stop Ollinger!

JACK DAKOTA

STOP OLLINGER!

Complete and Unabridged

LINFORD
Leicester

First published in Great Britain in 2012 by
Robert Hale Limited
London

First Linford Edition
published 2014
by arrangement with
Robert Hale Limited
London

A catalogue record for this book is available
from the British Library.

ISBN 978–1–4448–1849–9

Published by
F. A. Thorpe (Publishing)
Anstey, Leicestershire

Set by Words & Graphics Ltd.
Anstey, Leicestershire
Printed and bound in Great Britain by
T. J. International Ltd., Padstow, Cornwall

This book is printed on acid-free paper

1

The town of Mud Wagon Creek lay basking in the sun. A few people were about but generally things were quiet. Marshal Lou Burden sat on a chair outside his office with his hat brim pulled low and his feet on the rail in front of him. He was beginning to doze when suddenly he was roused by a distant rumble. *Thunder*, he thought; *not surprising in view of the type of weather we've been having.* He closed his eyes again. The thunder seemed to have rolled away into the distance when his ears picked up the noise again. *Thunder, like the beating of many hoofs.* Suddenly he jerked upright. It wasn't thunder he could hear; it was the sound of approaching horsemen, and lots of them. In an instant he had sprung to his feet and run inside his office.

'Hedley!' he shouted. 'Hedley!' His deputy appeared from a back room. 'Get your guns!' He stepped quickly to a gun rack and took down a Winchester '73 rifle which he snapped open and filled with shells from a drawer in his desk. Hedley came back with his own rifle held under his arm. 'Come with me,' Burden said.

They ran out into the street. Some of the passers-by had picked up the sound and stood in various postures with puzzled expressions on their faces. One young woman gathered up her child and ushered it along the boardwalk away from the ever growing volume of noise. A dog ran into the street and began to bark. Burden and the deputy marshal started to run and carried on till they reached the end of the street where the clapboards gave way to a few scattered adobes. Burden stationed himself in the middle of the road and gestured to Hedley to stand slightly behind him and to his left. He heard the sound of boots and looked round to see a couple of the townsmen running up carrying rifles.

'Go back!' Burden barked, but they shook their heads and took their stand beside him.

'Whoever those riders are,' one of them said, 'I reckon they sure as hell mean trouble.' He couldn't know the gang was led by Oregon Boot Bass Ollinger and he couldn't know how much trouble they were in.

A dense cloud of dust hung in the air as the ground began to shake with the thud of horses' hoofs. Then the riders came into view, galloping fast and whooping as they came. Some of them began to fire into the air, adding to the cacophony of noise which hurt the listeners' ears. They showed no sign of slowing and it seemed they must carry on and trample over the four men standing in front of them, when the leader held up his arm and they slowed. They were bunched but as they got close they began to spread out. The leader was almost up to Burden when he brought his horse to a rearing halt.

'Well now, if it ain't the town marshal,' he shouted. His words were greeted with sounds of laughter and hooting. A few more shots were loosed into the air.

'I don't know what this is about,' the marshal said, 'but I reckon you boys had best just turn right around and ride back where you came from.'

There was a moment's pause and then the leader, leaning over his horse's head, broke into a harsh laugh before replying. 'You hear, boys! The marshal would like us to turn round and go back where we come from.' There was further laughter and someone shouted: 'Better not mess with the marshal, Mr Ollinger.' Ollinger spat into the dust.

'You can see how it is, Marshal. My boys have ridden a long way and they were lookin' forward to a better reception. I don't think they're too impressed with the welcome.'

'This is a peaceful town. We don't want no trouble.'

4

Ollinger turned his head to his men. 'You heard the marshal. Now what do you think we ought to do?'

As his men responded with jeers and shouts a shot suddenly rang out and the marshal went spinning backwards. In the same instant, Ollinger spurred his horse and jerked forward, knocking the two townsmen aside. More shots rang out as the whole troupe of horsemen surged forward. The deputy marshal had his rifle in his hands and managed to squeeze off a couple of shots before he went down under the flying hoofs of the owlhoots' horses. The marshal rolled to one side, wincing with pain from a bullet to his shoulder, then began pumping lead into the galloping horde. Another bullet smashed into his leg. One of the townsmen was firing his rifle but the other lay in a crumpled heap.

The riders were now galloping down the main street of town, whooping and firing at anything that caught their attention. Windows shattered and bullets thudded into wood. Ricochets whined into the air and the whole scene was obscured by billowing dust and gunsmoke. The townsfolk who had been caught in the mayhem were running and screaming but there was nowhere for them to go. One of the owlhoots drew out his lariat and threw it in the general direction of the general store. It caught round a stanchion and, fastening the other end round the pommel of his saddle, he dug in his spurs. The horse pulled hard and the stanchion creaked and snapped. For a moment nothing happened but then one side of the building began to sag. A cloud of smoke billowed from one of the buildings and then a garland of flame rose into the air, crackling and hissing like a devil. The flames started to spread, slowly at first, but soon gaining in speed and intensity. Bodies were lying in the dirt. From the roof of the Bucking Horse saloon someone began to fire down on the gunslicks milling in the street below and soon shots could be heard issuing from some of the other buildings. The gunslicks began to spread out, some of them moving down the side streets and alleys, others dismounting, smashing down doors and entering buildings where people were hiding in terror. The woman who had ushered her child along the boardwalk was seized by a couple of the gunnies and carried kicking and screaming into the back of the millinery store. A group of gunnies burst through the batwings of the Bucking Horse saloon and began to fire at random.

Flames were spreading rapidly and most of the town was ablaze. The gunslicks threw blazing torches into the few buildings that remained unscathed as they ran along the street in a wanton rage of violence and destruction. A man burst from the saloon and began to run down the street but he didn't get far. Before he had managed a dozen yards he was run down by two horsemen and then seized by a group of the gunnies. It was a lynch mob now; they carried him through the open doorway of the livery stable and, fastening a lasso around his neck, hanged him from the ceiling.

Groups of townsfolk were fleeing into the fields surrounding the town and seeking whatever shelter they could among the trees. For most of them it was to no avail: Ollinger's gunslicks had a killing fever on them and pursued their quarry relentlessly. Most of the town centre was ablaze and buildings were collapsing in huge showers of sparks. A dense cloud hung over the place and through the swirling smoke Ollinger and his men flitted like devils, firing their guns randomly and destroying everything in sight. Ollinger sat astride his horse and observed the proceedings with a broad, ugly grin on his face. Mud Wagon Creek was just the first. There would be plenty of others. He was going to have a good time making people pay for what they had done to him.

When Marshal Burden came round from his faint, the first thing he was aware of was the pain in his leg and shoulder. An acrid smell filled his lungs and a sound like a multitude of snakes

8

filled his ears. Slowly raising himself so he was lying on one shoulder, he turned his head to see the still burning ruins of the town. He tried to stand but fell back grimacing with pain. He looked around for Hedley and saw him lying a short distance away in the dirt by the side of the road. Dragging himself along, he reached the deputy but it was immediately obvious that he was dead. He thought of the two townsmen who had come to their assistance. One of them lay mangled where the horses had trampled him into the dirt. He could not see the other one. He listened for sounds of shooting but they had ceased. Looking up at the sky, he realized that a considerable time must have passed since his initial confrontation with the gunslicks. His shoulder was hurting but his right leg was worse, although, as far as he could make out, it was not broken. But he had lost a lot of blood and needed help quickly if he was to have any chance of surviving. He began to pull himself along but every inch of progress seemed to cost an infinitude of pain; he had no idea how far he had slithered and crawled before darkness descended and he passed out once again.

It was a few days before the destruction of Mud Wagon Creek when Brant Forrest drew his buckskin gelding to a stop. It had been some hours since he had crossed the border and there couldn't be much further to go. He raised himself in the stirrups to take a good look around. The sun was going down but it was still hot and the air shimmered. The country was arid with just a few twisted cactus plants and yucca to relieve the harsh landscape. He took his bandanna and wiped the dust and sweat from his eyes, having to think for a moment before he remembered the name of the town he was looking for: Caldera. He had been south of the border before but hadn't come across it, not so far as he knew. It would probably prove to be just another anonymous fly-blown collection of wood and adobe shacks. There must be a church; he knew that because without a church there would be no icon and no reason for him to be there. He was getting tired and so was the horse. After thinking for a few more minutes he resolved to carry on a little further; if he didn't find the town then he would make camp for the night and carry on in the morning.

Darkness descended and he had not reached the village. Finding a suitable spot, he built a fire and made a meal of bacon and beans. When he had finished, he rolled a cigarette and reclined with his back propped against his saddle. The sky was filled with stars. By contrast with the heat of the day, the night was cold; when the fire had died down he wrapped himself in a blanket before stretching out with his rifle close at hand. Out in the darkness the buckskin snorted. He sat up and listened but his ears could detect nothing except the gentle soughing of the breeze. After a time he settled down to sleep but could not relax. Just beyond range of the firelight his horse stamped and blew. Something was making it restless. Abandoning his attempt to sleep, Forrest got to his feet and, taking his rifle, positioned himself in the shelter of some bushes from which he had a good view of the camp. He strained his ears in an effort to detect the slightest sound. His horse snorted once again and then quietness descended, a quiet deeper, it seemed, than what had preceded it. The tortured landscape glimmered in the moonlight; the raised arms of the saguaro cactus were transformed into the likeness of a man pleading his cause to the heavens but the only response was the unseeing eyes of a thousand stars. Forrest was still feeling twitchy but it seemed he had no cause. He was just about to step out of cover when the night's intense silence was shattered by the loud boom of rifle shots. Dust flew into the air as bullets bit into the earth and fluttered the blanket in which he

12

had been wrapped. Forrest swung his rifle in the direction in which he thought the shots had come and watched closely for any sign of his attacker. Nothing moved. He slipped back into the bushes and waited, hoping that whoever had fired the shots would turn up to check on the outcome, but no one appeared. When he felt certain that there was to be no follow-up and no repetition, he slid from cover and walked quickly to where he had been lying. There were several holes in his blanket. If he had stayed where he was he would almost certainly have been killed. He sat down out of the fire's glow and pondered the situation. Who could be responsible? And what reason could he have for wanting him dead? He could not come up with any answers. Maybe it was just some lone renegade; a bandit, a robber. But in that case, why hadn't he appeared to take his reward? He puzzled about it for a long time till, confident that his attacker had gone and of his own ability to waken at the presence of danger, he fell into a fitful doze.

He set off early the next morning and reached the village shortly before noon. He hadn't been wrong in his expectations. What passed as the main street was nothing but a dirt track on either side of which straggled a few roughly framed huts. Pigs wandered about and chickens flew up as his horse walked by, while a straggle of dirty children looked up at him with wondering eyes. At the end of the street a dusty plaza was surrounded on four sides by a motley collection of adobe buildings. On the fourth side stood the church, the only building in the whole place to show signs of care and attention. Its white-washed walls were surmounted by a square tower. As he swung down from the buckskin a bell began to peal. He looked about him. Some of the children had approached but still stood at a safe distance. A few older people had come out of their doorways and were also watching him. He became aware of an intermittent murmur from inside the church. He turned and, taking off his hat, walked through the door.

The interior was dark but illuminated in various places by candles. His nostrils picked up the smell of incense and as his eyes grew used to the dimness he could see several people kneeling in the pews. Some of them were mumbling words while their fingers picked at rosary beads. He suddenly felt conspicuous. It was a long time since he had been in church and he wasn't sure how to behave. He dipped his finger in the holy water and crossed himself before genuflecting awkwardly and taking a seat at the back. He sat quietly for a few moments before he remembered what he had come for and began to look around for the icon. Although he had been given a description, he wasn't altogether sure what he was looking for. He assumed it must be somewhere near the altar. His eyes swept the interior of the church, taking in the Stations of the Cross along the walls and the altar table with its silver monstrance. Beneath the mumble of voices at prayer, the church was filled with a deep silence. He became aware of someone watching him and glanced to his left. An old lady with a mantilla was looking towards him with a downward glance; he suddenly realized that he was wearing his six-guns. He made a move as if to unbuckle his belt but stopped and rose to his feet instead. Keeping to the shadows, he slipped back out of the door. After the gloom of the church, the sun struck him like a physical blow. He walked forward and, seeing a cantina more or less opposite, made his way across the plaza.

There was no door. He sat down at a rickety table on which stood a candle in a bottle. There was no one else in the cantina but after a moment a woman appeared from an opening leading to another room at the back. '*Sí señor*,' she said. 'What can I get you?'

'Copa of pulque,' he replied. The woman turned away and came back a few moments later with a jug and a green glass. She poured from one to the other. Forrest raised the glass. '*A su salud, señora*,' he said. She smiled.

'Would you like something to eat with it?'

'Enchiladas?'

She nodded and withdrew. Forrest swallowed the drink; it was thick but refreshing. He poured himself another and then sat back and stretched his legs. The woman came back with a plate of enchiladas. For a moment she hesitated, as if she was about to say something, but seemed to think better of it and walked away. While he ate he was thinking of what his next move should be when the doorway darkened and another person entered the cantina. Glancing at Forrest, he approached his table. 'Mind if I join you?' he said. Forrest pointed at a seat opposite him.

'My name is Father Dowd,' he continued. 'I am the village priest.'

Forrest looked closely at the new-comer. He wasn't dressed like a priest. He was small in stature and his cadaverous face was pock-marked and pitted with scars. 'I saw you enter and leave the church. If you don't mind my saying so, you look rather different from most of the people round here.'

'Most?' Forrest queried.

'I would have said all but for the fact that someone of a very similar type was here just a couple of days go.'

'So you would say that people fall into types?' Forrest said.

'I think you know what I mean. Another American, and carrying guns.' Forrest was interested but wasn't giving anything away.

'I saw you genuflect. Are you a Catholic?'

'Was once,' Forrest replied. 'A long time ago.' The woman had appeared from the back room and the priest looked up.

'Could I have some coffee?' he said. He turned back to Forrest. 'Maybe you

18

would like some too?'

'Sure,' Forrest replied.

When he had finished eating, Forrest drew a pouch of Bull Durham from his shirt pocket. He took out some tobacco and a paper and handed the pouch to the priest. When he had built a cigarette Forrest held a match to it. The priest inhaled. 'Thank you Mr Forrest,' he said. Forrest looked at him.

'I never mentioned my name,' he said.

'No, you didn't,' Dowd remarked, 'and I couldn't be certain that you and Forrest were the same. But when two men arrive in our village and they are both Americans and they both carry guns, I figure there's a connection. I heard your name from the other man I mentioned.'

'You didn't catch his name?' Forrest said.

'He told me his name was Brown. That seems a bit easy to me. I'd say it was something he made up on the spot. On the other hand, perhaps Brown is his name.' He paused for a moment. 'Or maybe he knew you were coming and didn't want you to know who he was.'

Whether it was real or not, it meant nothing to Forrest.

'And now let me tell you what you are doing in Caldera,' Father Dowd continued. 'You are here to look for the icon of the Virgin of the Sign.'

'You are very astute,' Forrest replied. 'Did you get that information from Brown too?' The sound of shuffling footsteps apprised them of the arrival of the woman with the coffee.

'Thank you, Isabella,' the priest said. The woman withdrew and Father Dowd proceeded to pour two mugs of coffee. He stubbed out his cigarette and took a drink. 'What I don't understand,' he said, 'is this sudden interest in the icon. You know, it's been around for an awful long time — since the seventeenth century, I believe. Its origin is uncertain. I don't know how much you know about these things.'

20

'Enough,' Forrest said. There was silence for a few moments.

'Would you like to see it?' the priest said. Forrest was taken aback. It was an invitation he hadn't expected. 'You were probably looking for it in the church. It isn't there. Oh, it used to be until very recently, but for the present I have removed it to a place of safe-keeping. In view of recent events, I'd say I was probably justified in taking precautions.'

'So why show me where you've hidden it?' Forrest said.

'Hidden isn't a word I would use in this context,' Father Dowd replied. 'Like I said, a place of safe-keeping sounds more appropriate. But in answer to your question; because for some reason I trust you and because I'd like to know just what this is all about.'

They finished the coffee and Forrest paid the woman. Leaving the cantina, they made their way back across the plaza to a low adobe building to one side of the church. The priest opened

21

the door and gestured for Forrest to go inside. He found himself in a narrow hall from which an open door led to what seemed to be a study. A man appeared from some inner recess.

'It's OK, Ignacio,' Father Dowd said. 'I have a visitor'. It was quite dark in the vestibule and Forrest could not clearly distinguish the man's features. He was tall, thin and slightly stooped and wore a drooping moustache.

'Will you be requiring anything, Father?' he said.

'No, just carry on with your duties. If I need you I will ring.' The man gave a sort of bow and moved away. 'That was Ignacio. He cooks for me and does some jobs around the place. To be honest, I could do without his services but he has sort of attached himself to me.'

Forrest nodded. The priest indicated the doorway to the study and Forrest preceded him inside. There was a leather-topped desk on which stood a jumble of books and papers, a couple of chairs and leather sofa. Two of the walls were lined with bookshelves crammed with books; on the third there was a map of the world while on the wall above the desk hung a crucifix.

'Take a seat,' Father Dowd said. Forrest did as the priest directed.

'Do you read at all?' Father Dowd asked. 'I'm afraid it is one of my vices.'

'There can't be much call for books round these parts,' Forrest commented.

'You are right. Most of these I have had with me for many years. They are beginning to show their age.'

Father Dowd sat at the desk and opened a drawer with a key he produced from a trouser pocket. He fumbled for a moment and then held up a small square object wrapped in oil-proof paper. 'Doesn't look like much, does it,' he said. 'I can't imagine what has caused you and Mr Brown to show such an interest.'

'So this man Brown was looking for it too?' Forrest said. 'Did you show it to him as well as me?'

'I did not. I'm afraid I did not have the same trust in him that I have in you.'

He carefully unwrapped the paper to reveal the icon. It was no more than eight inches high by four across and showed an image of the Virgin with her hands held out in prayer, wrapped in a blue robe; on her breast she wore a medallion in which the infant Jesus was depicted.

'The figure of Mary is of a type called the orans,' the priest continued, 'a style of image that goes back to the early years of Christianity. It depicts Mary and therefore the Church, since Mary is the image of the true Church, as a sign because of the presence of Christ within her.' He leaned across the desk. 'Here, take it and hold it. It is very beautiful, is it not?'

Forrest took the icon from the priest's hands and held it in the palms of his own. Looking at the image more closely, he felt strangely moved. After he had held it for a while he got to his feet and handed it back to Father Dowd. The priest gave it another searching look and then wrapped it and placed it back in the drawer, turning the key in the lock. He looked across at Forrest but did not say anything. Forrest felt an odd inclination to unburden himself to the little priest.

'Guess I owe you an explanation of what I'm doin' here,' he said.

The priest remained silent but continued to observe Forrest with a frank regard. 'Maybe a drink would help?' he said eventually. He got to his feet and walked across to a cabinet from which he produced a three-quarters full bottle of whiskey and two tumblers. He poured the drinks, handed one to Forrest, and sat down again.

'Let me take another guess,' he said. 'You were working on a ranch called the Wine Glass R.'

Forrest took a swallow of the whiskey and gave the priest a hard stare. 'You're good,' he said. 'How did you figure that one out?'

'Easy. The gentleman I mentioned — Brown — was riding a horse with a Wine Glass brand.'

Forrest grunted. 'Well, I guess that explains how he knew me, although I don't recall anyone of that name workin' on the ranch.' The priest was silent again.

'The Wine Glass is run by a man named Ringold,' Forrest continued. 'He runs one of the largest spreads in the Nueces River country and does a bit of collecting; paintings, pottery, that sort of thing.'

'And old icons?' the priest prompted.

'I guess so. He called me into his office one day and said he had a little job for me if I didn't mind doin' some ridin'. He said he had heard about a paintin' down Mexico way which he would like to add to his collection. He said it wasn't particularly valuable but that it might be worth preservin' as an historical item. I thought it seemed a bit odd but it was no skin off my nose to take a trip south of the border.'

'So you were commissioned to come down here and . . . ' Father Dowd paused for a moment. 'Acquire the icon.'

'That's about the size of it,' Forrest replied. Father Dowd took another sip of his whiskey. 'And how were you to acquire it?' he said.

'How do you mean?'

'Were you asked to pay for it or simply take it? Steal it, in other words.'

Forrest put his hand inside his shirt pocket and produced a crumpled wad of dollar bills. 'He gave me the money,' he said. 'But he made it clear he didn't care how I got it just so long as I did.' He leaned forward and laid the wad of money on the table. The priest picked it up and rifled through it.

'That's a lot of money,' he said. For some reason, Forrest felt uncomfortable.

'Why don't you count it?' he said.

The priest smiled and laid the roll of money down again. 'That won't be necessary,' he replied. 'You see, the icon is not for sale at any price. Oh, don't get me wrong. I don't imagine it is worth very much. But it's been here for a long time and it means a whole lot to the village folk and the farmers. In fact, I don't know what they'd do if the icon wasn't there.'

Forrest placed his drink on the floor beside him.

'So where does that leave you?' Father Dowd said. 'Seems to me, in view of what you've told me, that you only have one option. So why don't you just take it? I'm the only one here and I'm not likely to offer much resistance.'

Forrest sat deep in thought. Things weren't turning out quite as he'd expected. It would have been easy if he could just have ridden up to the church, seen the icon and taken it, leaving the wad of money behind in payment. That had been his intention. Now it was more complicated.

'It's not that difficult,' the voice of the priest broke in, as if he could read what he was thinking. 'After all, you've done everything that could be expected of you. You've found your way to Caldera and you've located the icon. It's not for sale. You don't owe Mr Ringold anything.'

Forrest got to his feet. 'I need to think about this,' he said. 'Is there anywhere in the village I can stay for a night?'

'There is, but you are welcome to stay right here.'

Forrest shook his head. 'I appreciate the offer, Father, but I kinda think it would be better if I stayed someplace else.'

'Then I would suggest you stay at Isabella's — you know, the lady who runs the cantina. She's got a room and I'm sure she'd appreciate the custom.'

'Thanks,' Forrest said. 'That sounds fine.' The priest got up to accompany him to the door. 'Thanks for the whiskey,' Forrest said.

'The pleasure's mine. A man gets tired of drinking alone.'

Forrest was about to ask whether the

priest should be drinking at all, but thought better of it. 'Will I see you tomorrow?' he asked instead.

'I'll be here,' the priest replied. 'Where else would I go? I'm easy to find.'

Forrest nodded and stepped into the sunlight. As he was about to walk away, the priest spoke again. 'There is one question you need to consider,' he said.

'I got a few questions,' Forrest replied. 'What you got in mind?'

'Mr Ringold trusted you with a lot of money. I suppose he resembles me in that regard. But since the icon has no particular value, why is he so keen to get his hands on it? He must be quite a connoisseur in these matters.'

Forrest felt slightly foolish. On the ride down to Mexico he had not given the issue any thought. He had been given a job to do and it wasn't for him to question the motives of his employer. He had been quite happy to get away from the ranch and spend time on his own. He had enjoyed the journey. Now he had talked with Father Dowd, the whole thing was in question. 'See what you mean,' he said.

He touched the rim of his Stetson and walked away across the sun-soaked plaza. As he did so he thought he could feel the priest's eyes on his back but when he glanced behind Father Dowd had gone. Another question the priest had raised worried him. What was Brown's role in the affair? Was Brown the man who had fired those shots and tried to kill him? He hadn't mentioned that incident to the priest, partly because it had not occurred to him that it might be connected with the business of the icon. Maybe it was just a coincidence, but it didn't seem likely now.

It was good to spend a night between sheets and when Forrest awoke the next morning he felt a lot better. He had barely slept the previous night and had been feeling the rigours of the journey down from Texas. Isabella's breakfast was just what was needed to complete his recuperation. He had finished eating and was enjoying a pot of thick black coffee when Father Dowd appeared in the doorway. Forrest could tell by his demeanour that something was wrong.

'Forrest,' the priest said. 'Do you have the icon?'

Forrest looked up at the priest's distraught features. 'Sit down,' he said. 'Have a cup of coffee.' The priest drew up a chair but did not take up Forrest's offer.

'I'm not sure I like what you're implyin',' Forrest continued.

The priest shook his head as if to rid his brain of the ragged thoughts that were occupying it. 'I'm sorry,' he replied. 'I said yesterday that I trusted you and I do.'

'You'd better tell me what's happened,' Forrest said.

The priest seemed to have calmed down a little. 'The icon is gone,' he said. 'I had breakfast and then went to my study. When I opened the drawer it wasn't there.'

'Are you sure? Maybe you looked in the wrong drawer.'

'I'm sure. The icon is gone. Whoever took it must have got in during the night.'

'Was the lock damaged? On the drawer, I mean.'

The priest shook his head. 'Not that I noticed.'

Forrest paused for a moment. 'Makes no difference,' he said. 'It wouldn't be hard for someone with any knowledge to get into it.'

'I should have realized,' Father Dowd muttered. 'I should have taken more precautions.'

'Why would you have done that? You had no real reason to suspect anything till I arrived, and that was only yesterday.'

'I should have taken a warning from Brown,' the priest replied. 'It's my fault.'

Forrest drank his coffee as Father Dowd lapsed into silence. After a few moments the priest spoke again.

'If the offer holds. I think I'll take you up on that coffee,' he said. Forrest called for another mug. 'That's better,' Father Dowd confirmed after swallowing a mouthful.

'I don't know what this is all about,' Forrest said, 'but it seems to me that Brown is the clue.' He proceeded to tell the priest about the attempted murder when someone had fired into his camping place. 'It's only a guess,' he said, 'but it's all we got to go on. This *hombre* Brown turns up asking about the icon. He apparently has a connection with the Wine Glass R. He seems to go away. A day or two later someone takes a shot at me. Now the icon has been stolen. I'd say, till we got anythin' better to go on, we start with Brown.'

The priest thought for a few seconds. 'You're probably right,' he said. 'But if you don't mind me saying, you seem to be assuming that we're somehow in this together.'

Forrest looked at him. 'Well, ain't we?' he said.

'You told me yesterday you wanted time to think about it.'

'That was yesterday. That was before what you just told me now.'

Father Dowd returned Forrest's look until a smile appeared at the corners of his mouth. 'Yes,' he said. 'You're right. I'd say we're both in this together.'

Forrest grinned in turn. 'Welcome, pardner,' he said, 'if that ain't bein' disrespectful, you bein' a priest an' all.'

'Forget about me being a priest,' Father Dowd said. 'Now, about this man Brown, he can't be far away if he stole the icon only last night.'

'That's what I was thinkin',' Forrest said. 'I reckon we should try and get on his trail. Maybe we can pick up his sign. Have you got a horse?'

'Certainly. A man called Miguel looks after it for me.'

'I got mine in a shed behind Isabella's. Go get your horse and meet me outside the church in half an hour.'

The priest got to his feet. 'I got a horse but I don't carry any guns.'

35

'Ain't that kinda risky?'

'There are dangers but people respect a priest. I haven't had any need to use one yet.'

'You ain't got no objections to my side irons?' Forrest said. 'I got a feelin' they might be needed.'

'You do what you think best. Every man has to make his own decisions.'

'Is that what the church teaches?'

'A man's conscience is the final arbiter,' Father Dowd replied.

In another moment he was gone. Forrest paid Isabella what he owed her and made his way to the shed behind the cantina. He saddled up his horse and stepped into leather. As he turned into the plaza, Father Dowd appeared, leading a rangy palomino.

'Are you sure you want to do this?' Forrest said. 'I mean, what about your flock? You must have plenty of things to do.'

'I can take the time,' Father Dowd replied. 'With any luck it won't take too long to track down this man Brown and

36

get the icon back. He can't be too far ahead of us.' He swung into the saddle. 'Which way?' he said.

'If Brown has anything to do with Ringold and the Wine Glass R, he'll probably head for the border. I'd say we ride in that direction.'

'That makes sense,' Father Dowd replied. 'Let's not waste any more time.' Spurring their horses, they rode down the dusty street away from the village.

They continued riding at a steady pace. As they went, Forrest was searching the ground for any indication of someone having passed that way a short time previously. There were various tracks, however, and he couldn't be sure whether any of them were those he was looking for.

'I don't suppose you happened to see what kind of a horse Brown was ridin'?' he asked.

'I'm sorry, I didn't,' the priest replied. 'Why, would it make a difference if you knew?'

'Probably not,' Forrest said. 'Tell me

again, how did you meet this *hombre* Brown?'

'I came across him in the church. He was looking at the icon. We talked.'

'What about?'

'I can't remember the details. It was a fairly desultory conversation till he touched on the topic of the icon. He said he had been admiring it and would I consider selling. I said that of course I wouldn't consider it.'

'How did my name come up?'

'He asked me if anyone else had shown any interest in the icon, and that's when he mentioned your name in particular. After that, I half expected you to turn up so I wasn't exactly surprised when you did.'

'What did he look like?'

'There was nothing distinctive about him that I can remember.'

Forrest thought for awhile. 'I got an idea,' he said. 'From what I can make out, Brown was at least as interested in me as in getting his hands on that icon. He wanted to check if I'd been in

Caldera. When he heard from you that I hadn't he decided to take me out of the picture by dry-gulchin' me. He must have lain in wait and when he thought I was asleep he shot me. At least, he thought he had. Then he came back to the village and stole the icon.'

'That sounds feasible except for one thing. How did he know where I'd hidden the icon?'

'That could be explained,' Forrest said. 'Before he left Caldera he went back to the church and noticed that the icon had been removed. He might even have seen you do it. It wouldn't take much thought to figure out where you probably hid it.'

'Do you think he could be working for this man Ringold?' the priest said. 'He said that's where he knew you.'

'He must have been ridin' for the Wine Glass otherwise there'd be no way he could have known about Ringold sendin' me down to Mexico. I don't think Ringold sent him after me — besides, it looks like he set out

39

before I did. Most likely he's operatin' on his own.'

'In that case, he isn't likely to be going back to the Wine Glass R.'

Forrest stroked his chin. 'Guess you're right,' he said. 'But that still leaves the question of where he is headed.'

'Could be we're going the wrong way after all.'

'I don't think so. He'd be more likely to aim for the United States than head deeper into Mexico.' Forrest looked ahead of him. The trail they were following was barely noticeable but it seemed to be different from the one he had ridden in on.

'I got an idea,' he said. 'Brown obviously wanted me out of the way. He thinks he has achieved that. He won't expect anyone to be comin' after him. He knows you're suspicious or you wouldn't have moved the icon, but he won't imagine you'd take the time to pursue him. He's probably pretty relaxed right now thinkin' he's in the clear. What I'm thinkin' is that if we ride hard we can get ahead of him. My guess is that he won't stop till he gets over the border, but once he does, he'll make for the nearest town. That's a place called Mud Wagon Creek. If I ride for the place and then make myself conspicuous, it might just be enough to draw him out.'

'Make yourself a target?' Father Dowd said. 'Make him come to you?'

'That's about the strength of it. It ain't much of a plan but it might just work.'

'I notice you said I rather than we at the end there,' the priest replied.

'If the plan has any chance of workin', Brown has to believe I'm on my own.'

'So what do I do?'

'There's a disused timber and sod dugout a few miles west of the town. I'll meet you there. If I've succeeded in flushin' out Brown, all well and good. With any luck I'll have the icon back again. If not, we'll need to do some rethinkin'.'

'How do I know I can rely on you to give the icon back? If you find it.'

Forrest grimaced. 'You were the one said you trusted me.'

'I'm sorry. I do trust you. Don't spend too long about this. At some point I'll need to get back to Caldera.'

'Make it the day after tomorrow,' Forrest replied.

They rode on silently till Forrest had a sudden thought. 'It just struck me; we're both devotin' a lot of time to this,' he said. 'That's kinda strange when you think about it. After all, you told me the icon isn't worth anything.'

Father Dowd smiled. 'Maybe we're both re-learnin' an old lesson,' he said.

'Oh yes. What's that?'

'That what a thing's worth ain't necessarily measured in money.'

Forrest pondered the priest's words. 'Hell,' he said, 'I think you just delivered your first homily.'

2

After camping for the night, Forrest and Father Dowd crossed the border early the next morning. Then they split up, Father Dowd following Forrest's instructions on how to get to the shack, and Forrest continuing along the trail that would bring him to Mud Wagon Creek. As he rode he kept on the lookout for any sign of Brown. One or two riders crossed his trail as he approached the town but there was nothing out of the ordinary about them. The first buildings arose abruptly out of the plain and in a moment he was riding past the worn clap-board false-fronts. Stopping outside the Bucking Horse saloon, he slid from the saddle. A few horses were tied to the hitchrack and he stooped to examine their markings. One of them bore the Wine Glass brand. *Hell*, he thought, *this is going to be easier than*

I'd imagined. Fastening the horse, he stepped through the batwing doors.

The place was quiet. A few people sat at the tables and one man, wearing a buckskin jacket, leaned against the bar, his foot resting on the rail. As he strode forward, Forrest looked in the mirror at the man's reflection. The man glanced up; there was no mistaking his sudden look of startled recognition. He spun round as Forrest came up behind him.

'Hello, Cushman,' Forrest said. 'Or should I say, Brown?'

'Forrest!' the man gasped. 'What the . . . '

Forrest grinned. 'Now, ain't this a surprise,' he said. 'I never expected to meet no one from the Wine Glass this far south.' He glanced at Cushman's glass. 'Two more whiskies,' he said to the barman. When the bartender had poured the drinks, Forrest addressed Cushman. 'Let's take a seat. I think you and me got some talkin' to do.'

Cushman hesitated for a moment

44

and then turned as if to pick up his drink. Forrest had taken the bottle in one hand and was about to pick up his own glass with the other when Cushman's hand suddenly fell towards his holster. Quick as he was, Forrest was quicker. In an instant he had drawn his six-gun and held it to Cushman's chest.

'You should have waited till I had the glass too,' he said. Cushman's face had blanched. 'Hand your gun to the barman,' Forrest said. 'Butt first.'

The bartender took Cushman's proffered weapon, glancing from one to the other as he did so.

'Now, like I was sayin', let's you and me go sit down and have a quiet talk.' Cushman shuffled his way to a table in a corner.

'Not that seat,' Forrest said. 'I want to see exactly what you're doin'.'

Cushman took the chair Forrest indicated. 'What are you expectin' me to do?' he said. 'You're the one with the gun.'

Forrest topped up their drinks. 'OK,'

he said, 'start talkin'.'

'Start talkin' about what?' Cushman said. 'I don't know what this is all about.'

Forrest took his gun back out of its holster where he had replaced it.

'You don't scare me,' Cushman said. 'You wouldn't use that thing. Not in here.'

'Is that so?' Forrest said.

'You wouldn't?' Cushman repeated, but this time it was more of a question than a statement.

'Maybe you and I should take a walk over to the marshal's office,' Forrest said.

'You can't pin that shootin' on me,' Cushman said. 'Besides, it weren't on United States territory.'

'What shootin'?' Forrest replied. 'I never mentioned no shootin'.' He picked up the gun and spun the chamber.

'OK, OK,' Cushman stammered. 'I admit it was me took those shots at you. But I didn't know it was you. I

46

thought it was somebody different.'
Forrest looked unconvinced.

'Look, I swear that's true. I thought I was gunnin' for someone else.'

'That don't excuse nothin',' Forrest said. 'Whoever you were aimin' for, it was a low-down stinkin' act of a skunk.'
Cushman shifted in his chair and then finished off his whiskey with one big swig. Forrest poured him another.

'Look, I ain't denyin' what you say. But you got to believe it wasn't you I was gunnin' for.'

'Then how do you know that it was me?'

'You said — '

'I didn't say nothin'. Seems to me like you're jumpin' to conclusions.'

'But I thought . . . it just seemed obvious it must have been you. How else would you have known about it? Why would you be here holdin' that gun?'

'It was me,' Forrest snapped, 'and you'd better have a mighty convincin' story.'

Cushman took another swig of whiskey. 'Don't suppose you got a cigarette?' he said.

'Sure.' Forrest handed him the makings. 'Right, now talk,' he said.

Cushman rolled a tight cigarette and lit up. 'Have you heard of a man called Ollinger?' he said. Forrest shook his head.

'You might know him better as Oregon Boot Bass.'

Forrest grunted. 'Oregon Boot Bass! His surname is Ollinger?'

'Yeah. Bass Ollinger. You know the story about how he got his name; because of the time he spent in the Oregon State Penitentiary? He had to wear a heavy iron shackle attached to the heel of his boot. It crippled him so that even when he got out he was never able to walk properly.'

'Yeah, I know all that. What's he got to do with it?'

'When he came back to Texas, he went into the cattle business. The way he did it was mostly by roundin' up

48

strays and puttin' his brand on them, but he wasn't averse to the odd bit of cattle rustlin'.'

'And that's when you met him, I suppose?'

'Yeah. He went on to set up the Grand Springs ranch in the Brasada.'

'I know it,' Forrest said. 'Who doesn't? So Oregon Boot Bass is the owner of the Grand Springs. That's a big spread. A lot bigger than the Wine Glass.'

'Sure is. But I can tell you that the money for the Wine Glass came from the same source. Griff Ringold was Ollinger's right-hand man till they fell out.'

'So what were you doin' ridin' for the Wine Glass?'

'That was Ollinger's idea. You see, that icon belonged to Ollinger. It disappeared and he suspected Ringold of bein' behind it. I got work at the Wine Glass in order to check things out. That icon is worth a lot of money.'

'That's not what I heard. I heard the

icon was worth nothin' in particular.'

'Who told you that?'

'I'm not the one doin' the explainin', but since you ask, it was the priest at the church in the village of Caldera who told me.'

Cushman laughed. 'Father Dowd?' he said.

'Yes. I gather you met him. Before you bush-whacked me.'

Again Cushman laughed. 'Father Dowd,' he said. 'That's a good one. That varmint ain't no more a priest than I am. Dowd was another one of Ollinger's men. If I was surprised when I heard that Ringold was sending you down to Mexico in search of that icon, you can imagine how surprised I was when I met up with Dowd again and discovered he was now posin' as a priest.'

Forrest felt the same way, but he didn't want to show it. 'I don't believe you,' he said.

'Dowd must have taken the icon. Not Ringold.'

'Describe Father Dowd to me.'

'He's a little weasely man with a badly marked up face. He got that from smallpox.'

'You still haven't explained about the shootin'.'

'After I left Caldera I was followed. I figured it might be Dowd so I took cover and watched my back trail. Sure enough someone was trackin' me but it wasn't Dowd.'

'Who was it then?'

'I don't know. It wasn't someone I recognized, but I'd have known if it was Dowd. So I waited till it was night and . . . well, you know the rest.'

'Didn't give him — me — much of a chance, did you? The fact remained you dry-gulched me like the ornery snake you are. It was just pure luck you didn't succeed in killin' me.'

'Like I say, I didn't know it was you.'

They lapsed into silence for a few moments. Forrest refilled Cushman's glass and poured a little for himself. Cushman finished his cigarette and

51

flicked the stub into a nearby cuspidor. 'What are you goin' to do now?' he asked.

'That depends. Where's the icon? Let me see it.' Cushman's face looked blank. 'Come on. Hand over that icon. I don't care whether it's worth anythin' or not. Either way, I want it.'

Cushman spread his hands in a gesture of baffled ignorance. 'I haven't got the icon,' he replied.

'Don't lie to me,' Forrest said. 'You went back and stole it.'

A look of innocence spread across Cushman's face. 'But I ain't got it. I never went back to the village. Once I figured someone was on my tail, I decided to wash my hands of the whole thing. It was startin' to get too complicated, too risky.' Forrest looked closely at him. Either the man was an excellent actor, or he was telling the truth.

'Are you tellin' me the icon's gone?' Cushman stuttered. 'Someone stole it from the church?'

'Not from the church. From Father

Dowd's desk in his study.'

'I swear it wasn't me,' Cushman said. 'You got to believe me.'

'I don't know who or what to believe,' Forrest said, 'but one thing you said I'm inclined to agree with; this icon has got to be worth somethin'. If not, why is everyone so interested in it?'

The whiskey bottle had gone down considerably. Forrest looked at the miserable figure of Cushman. He had had too much to drink and he looked a sorry sight.

'What are you plannin' on doin' with me, Forrest?' he said. Forrest realized that he really didn't know the answer to that question.

'Were you headin' back for the Grand Springs?' he asked.

Cushman shook his head. 'Nope. I don't know how Ollinger is goin' to take things.'

'You haven't done anythin' wrong so far as he's concerned.'

'Maybe not, but he might not see it that way.'

Forrest glanced at the gun which he had laid on the table. The gesture seemed to disturb Cushman even more than he was already. 'I got some more information that might interest you,' he said.

'Yeah? What would that be?'

'Promise you'll let me walk out of here. You won't regret it. You won't see me again.'

'I don't have to promise anythin',' Forrest said. 'But if you got somethin' to say, you'd better say it.'

It looked for an instant like Cushman was going to plead his cause again, but if that was the case he thought better of it. 'OK,' he said. 'I can't be exactly sure about this, but I'm pretty certain. Ollinger wants that icon, but not because it's valuable in itself. Rumour is that the icon holds the secret to the location of a hoard of treasure. Ollinger wants that treasure. He's already gathered together a whole bunch of *desperados* at the Grand Springs and they're just champin' at the bit.'

'Champin' at the bit? To do what?'

'Hell, it might be crazy, but Ollinger intends wagin' war on society for puttin' him in jail and makin' him wear that Gardner shackle. Maybe he'll even make it as far as Oregon.'

'You don't expect me to believe that?'

'Could be that Ollinger ain't right in the head, but it's what he's plannin'. That's why he wants that treasure. It's the prospect of strikin' it really rich that's holdin' 'em all together. Besides, with that kind of loot, Ollinger could afford not only to pay off those gunnies, but to buy up most of the other ranches as far as the Gulf Coast.' He paused before going on. 'If you've heard of Ollinger, you must have heard about some of the things he's done. I spent a good bit of time ridin' with him and for him. I know what he's capable of. That's why I ain't takin' no chance goin' back to the Grand Springs.' Forrest couldn't argue with that part of Cushman's story. Oregon Boot Bass had a nasty reputation and could be capable of anything. 'That's what I heard,' Cushman said. 'Now, will you let me go?'

Forrest gave Cushman a final hard stare. 'Once you walk out of here, you just keep right on goin',' he said. 'Don't get in my way ever again.'

'I won't. I'll go a long way from Texas. Believe me, you won't never hear from me no more.'

Forrest glanced towards the batwings. 'You'd better be right in what you've said,' he added, 'because if not, I'll make it a point of honour to hunt you down.'

'It's all true, I swear it. I've told you everythin' I know.'

'OK,' Forrest said. 'Get movin'.'

Cushman got to his feet and without looking back walked quickly out of the saloon. When he had gone Forrest poured himself a final drink, taking time to begin to assimilate what he had learned. When he had finished he stood up and, taking the empty bottle and glasses to the bar, threw some money on the counter. He turned away and had already begun to cross the room when the voice of the bartender called him back. 'Ain't you forgettin' something?' Forrest looked blank. 'That *hombre's* gun,' the bartender said. 'It ain't no use to me.'

Forrest strode back to the bar and the barman handed over Cushman's six-shooter. Forrest tucked it into his belt and walked away. When he stepped out on to the boardwalk the first thing he observed was that Cushman's horse had gone. Forrest felt pretty sure he wouldn't see the man again. Stepping down, he hoisted himself into the saddle of his buckskin and set off in the direction of the shack where he had arranged to meet Dowd.

While Forrest was dealing with his erstwhile henchman, the man known as Oregon Boot Bass was sitting on a luxurious leather settee in the main room of his spacious ranch house. In his hand he held an icon which bore some resemblance to the icon of the Virgin of the Sign. He turned it over. On the reverse side of the image the word *Berg* was scrawled in letters which the passage of time had rendered almost illegible. Getting to his feet, he replaced the icon in a safe and when he had done so he hung a painting over it to conceal it from a casual view. He took a moment to glance at the picture. Then he picked up a bell and rang it. After a few moments the figure of his cook appeared.

'Yes, Mr Ollinger?'

'Go on over to the bunkhouse and tell Rawlins to get in here.'

The cook went out and while he was fetching his foreman, Ollinger lit a cigar. When he had taken a few puffs the door opened and the chef came in, followed by the wiry frame of Rawlins. 'You wanted to see me, boss?' he said.

'Yes. Sit down. Have a cigar.'

Rawlins glanced round the room before seating himself on a chair at right angles to the settee on which Ollinger was seated. Ollinger handed him a cigar; he bit off the end and then lit it at Ollinger's proffered match.

'How long we been kickin' our heels here at the Grand Springs?' Ollinger said. It was a rhetorical question. Before Rawlins could say anything in reply, Ollinger continued. 'A long time. Too long. It's a good life but I ain't goin' to appreciate it properly till I've taken revenge for what they did to me in that penitentiary.'

'What are you sayin'?'

'I'm sayin' it's time we hit the trail. The men are ready. Why wait any longer?'

'Sure sounds a good idea to me. Some of the boys are out on the range. We'll need to decide who stays behind to work the ranch. How soon do we ride?'

'Don't see no point in hangin' around. How does tomorrow sound?'

Rawlins gave a loud laugh. 'Tomorrow sounds real good. Yup siree!'

Ollinger grinned. 'We're sure gonna have us some fun. They're gonna pay for lockin' me away and leavin' me with a limp. They ain't gonna know what's hit 'em.'

He left vague just to whom the word *they* referred. It left him a wide scope for raising hell. He and his foreman discussed some further details and then Rawlins left. Ollinger accompanied him as far as the veranda and sat down in a cane chair. Beyond the yard the land in front of him rolled away into the blue distance. He felt a glow of satisfaction suffuse him. As far as the eye could see and beyond it was all his, and this was just the start. All he wanted now was for Cushman to return. It could be any time. Maybe he would have the icon with him. If not, it might be worth taking a little detour and dealing with Ringold before setting out on the owlhoot trail, just on the chance that he was responsible for taking it. If he wasn't, what did it matter? He intended taking over the Wine Glass pretty soon anyway. The boys might appreciate the chance to let off a little steam. He would let things take their course and act according to how they turned out.

When Cushman left the Bucking Horse saloon and climbed into leather, he rode hard till he was well clear of town. Only when he had put some distance between himself and Mud Wagon Creek did he slow down and allow the horse to continue at its own pace. He was badly shaken and his one intention was to get way from Forrest. He had been sincere in his declaration that he did not intend to return to the Grand Springs, but as he rode on and his nerves steadied, he began to have second thoughts. Forrest was right. He had done nothing wrong. He had followed Ollinger's instructions by getting a job at the Wine Glass R and had tracked down the icon. What had he to fear from Ollinger? He had served Ollinger well enough in the past and had done quite well out of it. He had a comfortable berth at the ranch, so why should he leave it to face an uncertain future looking for something else to do, having to look for work on other ranches, becoming a wandering range bum? He wouldn't find anything better than what he already had. Then another thought struck him. He could tell Ollinger that Forrest had got to the icon before him and it was now in his possession. He couldn't be certain how Ollinger would take the news, but he could hardly be blamed for such an outcome. After all, Ollinger's instructions had not gone further than telling him to spy on things at the Wine Glass R. Finding that the icon was in Mexico and following Forrest to Caldera was an extra. And if the icon meant that much to Ollinger, he might well consider doing something about it. In fact, it seemed more than likely that he would. In that case, Forrest would have no chance of coming out of it alive and he, Cushman, would have his revenge. He would be rid of any lingering threat from Forrest. The more he thought about it, the better he liked it. A grim smile crept involuntarily across his features. Forrest had humiliated him.

He had given him a bad fright. Well, he would learn that it wasn't wise to meddle with Lloyd Cushman.

* * *

It was late in the afternoon when Forrest arrived at the sod cabin. Father Dowd's horse was cropping grass in a pasture in the rear. Forrest dismounted and led his own horse to the pasture, where he hobbled it. Then he moved to the front of the cabin and opened the door. Dowd was sitting astride a chair pointing a rifle at him.

'Well, this ain't exactly the kind of greetin' I was expectin',' Forrest said. 'I thought you said you didn't carry no guns.'

'Where's Brown?' Dowd replied.

Forrest pulled a face. 'I caught up with Brown but I didn't invite him along with me.' Dowd seemed to reflect on Forrest's words for a moment.

'Take off your gunbelt and drop it on the floor.' Forrest shrugged before following Dowd's instructions. Dowd gave him a searching look. 'Did you kill him?' he said.

Forrest gave a deep sigh. 'Look, I don't know what this is all about,' he said, 'but until you decide to enlighten me, do you mind if I take a seat?' Dowd nodded to a chair and Forrest sat down.

'Tell me what happened,' Dowd said.

'Before I do, would you mind puttin' that thing down and not pointin' it at me?'

Dowd lowered the rifle. 'Go on, start talking,' he said. Forrest began to tell him about his encounter with Cushman, but even before he was finished Dowd laid the rifle to one side.

'I'm sorry,' he said. 'I guess being on my own in this goddamned place got me spooked. I found this rifle in the cabin. It isn't loaded. Probably doesn't even work. I got to thinking about the arrangement we made and it began to seem a little odd. I figured that maybe there was something more to you riding off to find Cushman and telling me to wait here. I started to wonder if maybe you and Cushman were working together and the plan was just a ploy to get me out of the way. When I heard you coming up the trail, I figured maybe you had Cushman with you.'

'Well, you figured wrong,' Forrest replied. 'But now we're on about suspicions, I forgot to mention a little detail that Cushman told me.'

'Yes? What was that?'

'Cushman seems to think you ain't no more a priest than he is. In fact, he told me that far from bein' a man of God, you used to ride the owlhoot trail with Ollinger.'

Dowd's jaw tightened. 'He could have been lying,' he said.

'He could have been.'

The priest paused. He reached into a pocket and pulled out a hip flask. Unscrewing the top, he took a swig of whatever was inside and handed it to Forrest. 'Fact of the matter is, I trained to be a priest but left the seminary before being ordained.'

'So what about the rest of it? Is that true too?'

'If you mean, did I once ride with Ollinger; yes, I did. It's a common story. I got into bad ways. After Ollinger went inside the penitentiary and his gang broke up, I drifted around and ended up in Caldera. The rest just fell into place.'

'So all the time those villagers thought they had a priest to minister to them, they were mistaken?'

'I don't feel good about it,' Dowd replied. 'In fact, I feel downright sinful. I done some bad things in my time, but that's the worst.' Forrest got to his feet and began to pace the room. 'Well,' Dowd concluded, 'I guess there's nothing to be done about all that now. Right at this moment we got to think what we do about the icon. If Cushman hasn't got it, then who has?'

Forrest continued to prowl up and down, deep in thought. 'Maybe I was wrong to believe Cushman,' he said.

'Maybe we'd do best to just forget

about the icon,' Dowd replied. 'I should be getting back to Caldera.'

Forrest stopped in his tracks and burst into a hollow laugh. 'Get back to Caldera,' he repeated. 'What's so urgent about doin' that now? You were there under false pretences all along. It ain't as if the villagers are goin' to miss havin' a genuine priest.'

'They don't know the truth,' Dowd replied. 'So long as they think I'm a priest, maybe that's what matters.'

'Do you think you can carry on with the façade?' Forrest said.

Dowd looked crestfallen. He took another swig from the flask. 'No,' he said, 'I don't suppose I can.'

'It's up to you,' Forrest said. 'You can turn round and go back if that's what you want.'

'What do you intend doing?'

'I think I'll carry on to the Wine Glass. I reckon I owe it to Ringold to let him know what's happened. After that I might just pay a visit to Ollinger. Despite what he said about stayin' clear

67

of Ollinger, I wouldn't be surprised to find Cushman there. It might pay to have another discussion with the varmint.'

'You're still thinking about that icon? Why?'

'I don't like to let drop somethin' once I've started. Besides, I feel kinda responsible. If I hadn't agreed to the Mexico trip, maybe none of this would have happened and at least the villagers would still have their icon.'

Dowd stood up and slipped the flask back into his pocket. 'You're a strange one,' he said, 'but what you say makes sense, especially the bit about carrying on with the façade.'

Forrest had already forgotten his own words. 'Façade?' he said.

'Yes. All this time I've been fooling those folks. They put their trust in me. And it isn't as though I'd stolen something material from them. No, I've stolen something much more important, much more precious. I'll never be able to undo what I've done, but at least I can help get back that icon. In a small way I'll have started to repay them.'

'Does that mean you're comin' with me?' Forrest replied.

'Yes. If you'll still have me along. Later, sometime, I'll go back to Caldera and confess what I've done.'

'Would that be wise? They ain't likely to take the news too well.'

'It's something I'm going to have to do. Hell, my whole life's been a façade. Riding with those outlaws was a façade. I was young, I was confused, I was angry. I'm beginning to see it more clearly now.'

Forrest clapped him on the shoulder. 'I wish you well,' he said. 'Right now, I'll be glad to have you along. I reckon we might as well stay here overnight now and ride in the mornin'.'

Dowd nodded. 'You won't hear me moaning any more,' he said. 'Sit down and take it easy. I'll rustle us up something to eat.'

Ignacio Ramirez was only half Mexican. His father had been a Scotsman but Ignacio had never known him and had taken the name of the ranch dwelling and fort in Live Oak County, Texas, near which he had spent some of his early years. Like Father Dowd, his varied and chequered career had washed him up in Caldera and it was there that he had developed a devotion to the icon of the Virgin of the Sign. He had attached himself to Father Dowd when he came on the scene, and for the first time in his life he had enjoyed a period of relative peace and tranquillity. Now, with the arrival first of Brown and then of Forrest, that peace had been shattered and the thing he venerated had come under threat. And it was not just a vague threat; he recognized the man calling himself Brown from earlier times when he had been associated with Oregon Boot Bass Ollinger. There was obviously something behind Brown and

Forester's appearance in the quiet Mexican hamlet and it seemed Oregon Boot Bass Ollinger was involved. He had heard rumours about the icon and the stack of treasure it was rumoured to be associated with. He didn't care about the treasure but he did care about what might happen to the icon. He was faced with difficult choices.

The icon had been removed from the church and placed by Father Dowd in his drawer, but was it really safe there? The more Ignacio thought about it, the more it seemed that it would only be secure when it was in his keeping. To take it from Father Dowd's drawer was easy, but what was he to do next? His first inclination had been to leave Caldera with it and ride somewhere deep into Mexico where no one would be likely to find either him or the icon. But then, Brown and Forrest had found their way to Caldera. If he simply fled somewhere, he could never be certain that someone wouldn't come looking for the icon again and find him. He racked his brains, trying to decide what was the best thing to do. The more thought he gave to it, the more it seemed to him that the only way for the icon to be safe would be to find out what Ollinger was up to and somehow put a stop to it. He didn't know what that would involve, but he needed to know what Ollinger's game was. And the first step in that direction was to find Father Dowd and the stranger he had ridden off with. He felt badly about deceiving Father Dowd, who had been good to him in the past. Father Dowd was wise; he would know the best course of action to follow. He debated whether to leave the icon somewhere behind, but he knew he wouldn't be able to rest easy unless he knew it was safe, and that meant carrying it with him. After all, it had protected him so far and would surely continue to do so. No harm would come to him while it was in his keeping and he was active in its service. Once he had taken the icon from Father Dowd's drawer to meditate and pray over it, he felt the old, familiar calm come over him; the pangs of conscience he felt about taking it were stilled. He spent the long dark watches of the night in contemplation and when he rode out the next day for Texas he felt better about the whole affair; purposeful and steeled to his mission.

It was late in the morning when Forrest and Dowd finally left the cabin. They rode slowly through brush country with thick sections of mesquite and chaparral in the direction of the Nueces River. Flies rose in clouds about their heads and their horses' tails flicked. The air was heavy with heat and several times Forrest wiped the sweat from his brow with his bandanna. They stopped by a stream to let the horses drink. As they were about to climb back in the saddle, Forrest noticed a vague cloud on the horizon. He pointed it out to Dowd.

'I'd say that cloud was caused by riders,' Forrest said. 'And a lot of them.'

'What do you reckon they're doing?' Dowd asked.

'I don't know, but it looks like they're headed this way and I don't like it.'

They climbed into leather and began to ride. Forrest was looking for a place where he could get a decent view of the riders through his field glasses and after a time they saw a small mound and rode to the summit. They dismounted and Forrest put the glasses to his eye. The riders were still quite a long way off and the dust they were raising rendered visibility difficult. He handed the glasses to Dowd who took a long look before putting them down.

'They are definitely heading this way,' he said. 'I reckon there must be well over twenty of them.' Forrest took up the glasses again. Suddenly he gave a jerk. 'What is it?' Dowd snapped.

'Unless I'm very mistaken, one of those riders is Cushman,' he replied. 'And there's something familiar about some of the others. I ain't had a lot of dealin's with the Grand Springs ranch, but I think I recognize some of their riders.'

74

Dowd peered through the glasses again. 'It's been a long time since I saw him,' he said, 'but I'd be willing to bet that the one at the front is Oregon Boot Bass.'

'Ollinger!' Forrest snapped. 'Now what the hell would Ollinger and his men be doin' away from the Grand Springs?' They looked at one another with consternation written on their features.

'Didn't you say Cushman told you he was gettin' ready to start out on the owlhoot trail again? Well. Looks to me like he has.'

Forrest made a fist and thumped the air. 'Hell, you're right,' he said. 'And if Cushman's with them, there's a good chance they're startin' with us.'

'How do you mean?'

'Cushman said he wasn't goin' back to the Grand Springs. Obviously he lied, or he changed his mind. Now why would Ollinger be headed for Mud Wagon Creek? What reason would he have other than to catch up with me? I bet it's got somethin' to do with that icon.'

'But Cushman said he didn't have it.'

Forrest was thinking hard, trying to make sense of the new situation. 'I've got it,' he said. 'He probably told Ollinger that I've got the icon. Either that or he had the icon all along and Ollinger wants to put me out of the reckoning.'

'Seems to me like you're making some presumptions there,' Father Dowd said. 'It could just be chance that Ollinger is heading this way.'

Forrest shook his head. 'No. It would make more sense for him to head north. Especially if he was mad enough to think about ridin' all the way to Oregon. Cushman seemed to think he might do just that.'

'If you're right, things seem to have got mighty unhealthy.'

'They sure have. It ain't gonna take Ollinger long to get on our trail.'

'So what do we do?'

'We could carry on to the Wine Glass

but I don't want to bring Ollinger and his boys down on Ringold's head.'

'Back to Mexico?' Dowd said.

'Not that either, and for the same reason. I reckon we wait for a while and then head for Mud Wagon Creek.'

'Why Mud Wagon Creek? Didn't you just say that's where Ollinger and his gang are headed?'

'That's exactly why we should make it our first stop. Ollinger or some of his boys are bound to talk. We might be able to pick up a few clues about their intentions, and not just with regard to us. We might even be able to discover whether he has that icon.'

'I suppose you know what you're doing' Dowd said, 'but I'll tell you something. If I remember Ollinger right, he's capable of riding into that town just for the pure joy of raising hell. And if he's looking for us, there won't be any chance of avoiding him; he'll find us sooner or later.'

3

Long before Forrest and Dowd arrived at the town of Mud Wagon Creek, the acrid smell of burning reached their nostrils. As they got closer they could see lingering spirals of smoke ascending.

'What do you think?' Dowd said.

'Same as you. Oregon Boot Bass. It couldn't be anyone else. Looks like his campaign of hate has started already.'

They rode past houses and buildings on the outskirts of town that were untouched, but as they approached the centre hardly a single building had survived unscathed. Many were razed to the ground and those that still stood were burnt and scorched. In several places, people were still pouring water on the smouldering remains. They looked up at the two riders with fear on their faces. Forrest and Dowd dismounted and fastened their horses to a blackened hitch rack.

'What happened?' Forrest said to a man standing nearby with a bucket in his hands.

'A bunch of outlaws. We didn't do nothin' to deserve it,' he replied. Forrest and Dowd exchanged glances.

'Where can I find the marshal?' Forrest said.

'He's been hurt. He's over at what's left of Doc. Johnson's.'

Following the man's directions, they made their way past burnt-out, smouldering buildings. The doctor's house was in a more residential area of the town which had escaped the worst ravages of the flames and was easily recognizable by the number of injured people moving in and out. They were about to walk up the path when a voice rasped out: 'Reach!' Forrest's hand dropped towards his holster.

'I wouldn't do that,' the voice said.

Forrest turned his head. Two men had just come up behind them and both carried rifles.

'What is this?' Forrest said. A couple

more men came out of the house, six-guns in their hands.

'Better drop your gunbelts,' the voice said. Forrest did as he was bid. Dowd indicated that he wasn't wearing one. The two men who had come out of the building began to frisk them, after which one of them nodded.

'Go right on in, gentlemen,' the voice ordered.

Preceded by two men and with the other two at their rear, they entered the building. Seated on a wooden chair, distinguished by his badge of office, sat the marshal, his thigh and one arm swathed in bandages. He looked up at their approach.

'Hello,' he said. 'What's this?'

'We caught these two *hombres* outside. They were comin' this way. Figured they might have somethin' to say about what happened.'

The marshal looked them over. Despite his wounds, his eyes were sharp and bright. 'Well?' he said. 'Have you?'

Forrest sighed. 'Look,' he replied, 'it's

pretty clear what's happened here, but if you think we had anythin' to do with it, you're wrong.'

'You got to admit it's a bit of a coincidence you two showin' up right now. We don't usually get a lot of strangers passin' through.'

'If we had any part in this, do you think we'd still be hangin' about? What reason would we have for bein' here?'

'I don't know. You tell me.'

'I swear we ain't involved, but I got a pretty good idea who is responsible.'

'Who says anybody is responsible? Coulda just been a fire.'

'You made it pretty obvious it wasn't.'

The marshal's face relaxed. He turned to the men who had brought them in. 'Good work, boys,' he said. 'Leave this to me. Go and see if the doc wants any more help.'

Giving Forrest and Dowd unmistakably suspicious looks, they moved towards a door at the back of the room beyond which figures could be seen

81

moving. 'We'll be right on hand if we're needed,' one of them said.

When they had gone, the marshal turned to Forrest. 'OK,' he said. 'Tell me who is responsible and just how come you have that information.'

'I'd appreciate havin' my guns back first,' Forrest said.

The marshal nodded and Forrest picked up his gunbelt from a table where it had been laid. The marshal looked curiously at Dowd.

'I don't carry guns,' Dowd said.

Forrest fastened his belt round his waist. 'Let us introduce ourselves,' he said. 'My name's Forrest and until recently I rode with the Wine Glass R. You might know it?'

'Yeah, I know it,' the marshal said. 'And this is . . . ?'

Forrest hesitated for a moment. 'Father Dowd,' he added. Again, the marshal gave Dowd a curious glance before informing them of his own name.

'I'm Burden,' he said. 'Lou Burden.

82

I'd appreciate any information you boys might have about what occurred here.'

Keeping his explanation as brief as possible, Forrest told the marshal what they knew of Ollinger and his doings. When he had finished, the marshal stroked his chin.

'Kinda strange, a priest bein' mixed up in all this,' he remarked.

There was no reply from either Forrest or Dowd and the marshal soon continued, not bothering to follow up his own comment.

'What you say kinda makes sense,' he said. 'The Grand Springs ranch ain't so far away that I haven't had a few suspicions about some of the things that seem to be goin' on there. But I can't believe anybody would go to these lengths.'

'You don't know Ollinger,' Dowd said. 'The man's insane. They did more than damage his leg when they strapped that boot on him.'

The marshal began to struggle to his feet with the aid of a stick. Dowd moved across to help him. 'Those stinkin' varmints shot me down in cold blood,' he said. 'But they ain't gonna get away with it. No, not for what they did to me or this town. They're gonna pay; just as soon as I can get back on a horse, they're gonna pay.'

'Take it easy, Marshal,' Forrest said. 'You ain't in any condition to be overdoin' things at the moment.'

The marshal leaned on his stick, quivering with rage and exhaustion. Just at that moment a man emerged from the other room. 'What are you tryin' to do?' he said to the marshal. 'You shouldn't even be out of bed.' He looked at Forrest and Dowd.

'This is Doc Johnson,' Burden said. The doctor was tall and lean; his face was lined with tiredness and there were bloodstains on his crumpled white shirt.

'If you two want to help,' he said when the introductions had been concluded, 'there's plenty work to be done.'

Forrest and Dowd exchanged glances. 'Sure,' Forrest said. 'We'd be happy to oblige. We might not be much use on the medical front, but I guess there's plenty other things need attendin' to.'

'I can help with the medical side, if that would be any use,' Dowd interposed. 'Workin' as a priest carries a lot of other responsibilities with it.'

The marshal looked from one to the other of them. 'Unless you boys are in a hurry to get off,' he said, 'why don't you try bookin' in at Louisa Dolan's eatin' house? Sorry, but there ain't much left of the hotel.'

'Sounds fine,' Forrest said. 'Where do we find it?'

'I need to get some supplies from the store,' the doctor said. 'Why don't I show you where it is on the way?' He turned to the marshal. 'I'll be right back,' he said. 'Don't you try and do anythin' stupid while I'm gone.'

* * *

85

Oregon Boot Bass Ollinger and his men were celebrating the destruction of the town of Mud Wagon Creek. They had looted supplies of beer and whiskey and the empty prairie rang with shouts and laughter and the occasional bark of a gun. Flames from their camp-fires shone into the night.

'Hell, that sure was some fun,' his foreman Rawlins exclaimed.

'Yeah. And it's just the start,' Ollinger replied.

Rawlins took a swig from a bottle he held in his hand. 'What next, boss?' he said. 'We gonna burn out that varmint Ringold?'

Ollinger seemed to consider the question. 'No,' he said. 'Leastways, not for the moment. Ringold can wait. We got more important things to do first.'

'Are we goin' after that treasure hoard you were tellin' us about?'

Again Ollinger seemed to consider the matter. He was beginning to wonder whether it had been altogether wise to mention it to any of them. It only served to raise expectations. A short way off Cushman was sitting in the firelight.

'You sure about this Forrest *hombre?*' Ollinger shouted.

Cushman got to his feet and lumbered over. 'What's that you say, boss?'

'I said are you sure that Forrest has the icon?'

Cushman looked blank. He had drunk a lot and he failed at first to understand what Ollinger was talking about.

'The icon,' Ollinger snarled.

The tone of Ollinger's voice brought Cushman to his senses. 'The icon. Yeah, I'm sure. Forrest has it.'

Ollinger continued to stare at his henchman with contempt in his eyes. 'You'd better be right,' he said.

Rawlins spat into the fire. 'So all we got to do is find Forrest,' he said.

'That would seem to be the case,' Ollinger said. 'And from what Cushman has told us, he can't be far away. But there's time enough for that. Before we find Forrest, I got a little somethin' else in mind.'

Rawlins couldn't hide the excitement in his face. 'What is it?' he said. 'We gonna burn us another town?'

'Yeah, we might do that. But our target is the bank.'

Rawlins let out a whoop which brought a few of the others running up. 'Which bank?' Rawlins asked.

'The Third National at Stinkweed.'

Rawlins whooped again and this time he was joined by some of the others. 'When do we do it, boss?' somebody shouted.

'It'll take nearly two days to get there,' Ollinger said. 'So make the most of things tonight. We got some hard ridin' in front of us.'

He got to his feet and limped away, leaving his boys cheering and hallooing in his wake. None of them followed him. They knew better than to disturb their leader when he wanted to be alone and they knew that time had come. Among the trophies he had carried away from Mud Wagon Creek was a young girl he had swept up as she walked down the street. And he wasn't the only one to have done so.

By the time they had finished for the day, Forrest and Dowd were exhausted. They had spent the time helping to tidy up the mess. The centre of town had been gutted and it would take a long time to rebuild, but the townsfolk were already making a start. The mood was grim and some of the towns-people had been reluctant to accept their assistance but they soon proved their worth. When they eventually got back to the boarding house they found a warmer welcome. Although they were the only residents, Louisa had not spared in her mealtime arrangements.

'I figured you boys would be hungry,' she said.

'You shouldn't have gone to such lengths,' Forrest replied, 'but we sure appreciate it.'

When the food was served, Forrest looked across at Dowd, half expecting him to say grace, but he showed no inclination to do so. When they had finished, they went out on to the veranda to smoke.

'Sure is a nice lady,' Dowd remarked.

For a moment Forrest was uncomprehending. 'Miss Dolan? Yeah, she's done us proud. Especially in view of the circumstances.'

They fell into silence, drawing on their cigarettes, when they heard the sound of footsteps and Miss Dolan herself appeared carrying a tray on which were two mugs and a pot of coffee.

'Would you care to join us?' Dowd said.

The woman looked as if she was about to refuse but then changed her mind. 'If you don't mind,' she replied. 'I think right now I could do with a bit of company.'

She went to get an extra mug and then rejoined them. Dowd poured her a cup of the hot steaming liquid. 'It's a terrible thing, what happened here,' he said.

'I understand you spent the afternoon helping to clear things up. That was good of you.'

'It's the least we could do. We'll be happy to do the same tomorrow.'

'Are you intending to stay for long?'

'We can afford to stick around for a day or two,' Forrest said, 'if we can be of some use.'

'Are you visiting or just passing through?' she asked.

'Just passin' through,' Forrest replied.

She seemed to accept the answer but Forrest suddenly felt that further explanation was required. 'I work for a ranch called the Wine Glass R,' he said. 'My friend has business in the area. It involves a man by name of Cushman. He was in the town of Mud Wagon Creek quite recently.'

Although the original impetus behind his comment had not been to try and elicit any possible information about Cushman, Forrest found himself mentioning the name. But if he had hoped for any response, he was disappointed.

'Cushman,' she repeated. 'No, I don't know the name.'

'He might be callin' himself Brown,' Forrest remarked.

'Certainly no one called Cushman or Brown has stayed here. To be truthful, business had been slack recently. Have you tried the hotel?'

'The hotel's in a bad way,' Dowd replied. 'But we'll certainly make inquiries.'

As Dowd spoke, Forrest was thinking of how ironic it was that they had come to Mud Wagon Creek to try and discover something of Ollinger's intentions. There were no doubts about them now.

'I've never known anything like this before,' Miss Dolan said, alluding once more to what had happened. 'It's terrible. This has always been such a peaceful town; especially since Mr Burden took over as marshal. From what I understand, it was a miracle he survived, never mind trying to get about with a stick. He was shot twice, poor man.'

'The marshal seems to be making a

good recovery,' Dowd said.

Forrest was about to say something about what had happened to some of the other citizens, but did not do so. He wasn't sure just how much the good lady knew about events.

'I suppose it's too late to get up a posse?' Miss Dolan continued. 'Even if the marshal was in a fit state to ride.'

'I wouldn't worry about that,' Forrest said. 'A big bunch of riders will be sure to have left a trail. In fact, when Father Dowd and myself have done what we can here in town, I reckon we'll see if we can locate the varmints ourselves. With or without a posse.'

Miss Dolan looked surprisingly alarmed. 'But there's only two of you,' she said. 'What could you be expected to do?'

Forrest looked into her anxious green eyes. 'We can take care of ourselves,' he said. 'Whatever it takes, those gunslingin' coyotes aren't gonna get away with it.'

★ ★ ★

The town of Stinkweed was growing in importance. It was already on a regular stage route and there was talk of a spur line linking it with the main railroad. The bank seemed to reflect its developing status; it was big and square and dominated a corner of the main street. Inside his plush office, the bank manager, Mr Meeker, was taking a few moments away from a pile of papers on his desk to take a look through the blinds at what was happening on the street below. He smiled with satisfaction. It was an ordered scene; as he glanced up and down, he recognized all the names on the front of the buildings just as he did most of the people passing along the walkways. A buckboard passed below his window and turned into a side street. A woman paused, holding her hat, while a horseman trotted by. The sounds of the street drifted up to his window like wisps of smoke, oddly comforting. He turned back to his desk and began to rifle through his papers, pausing occasionally to sign a document with a gold pen. A fly buzzed. He leaned back in his chair, feeling sleepy.

He must have drifted off because he was awakened by a sudden bustle of activity and noise which seemed to come from the main body of the building on the other side of his door. A voice rose but he couldn't hear what was being said. Slowly, he got to his feet but before he reached the door it flew open and he was confronted by a man with a mask pulled up to his eyes. It was the last thing he ever saw. As he opened his mouth to speak the intruder raised a gun and fired three shots. Mr Meeker clutched his stomach and then fell to the floor; a pool of blood began to gather about him as he twitched once, twice and then died. The killer rushed to the desk from which he pulled a bunch of keys. He ran out the door. Someone screamed and then there was a burst of gunfire from the street. It was the diversion Ollinger had arranged to take place outside the saloon, happening right on time. Smoke began to rise from the direction of the livery stables. There was a fresh commotion, panic on the streets and the sound of galloping horsemen, but neither Mr Meeker nor his bank were any longer concerned. Oregon Boot Bass Ollinger had struck again.

★ ★ ★

It was the evening of the second day of their stay in Mud Wagon Creek that Forrest and Dowd received a visit from Marshal Burden. To their surprise, and that of their hostess, he had cast away both the bandages and the crutch.

'I hear you boys been doin' some good work around the town,' he said.

'Just happy to have been able to help,' Forrest replied.

Miss Dolan looked at the marshal disapprovingly. 'You'll not do any good tryin' to rush things,' she said.

Burden turned to her and smiled. 'Appreciate your concern,' he said, 'but I'll be fine. Things weren't as bad as the doc made out. I still got some stiffness but I reckon I'm ready to get back into harness.'

'I guess a cup of coffee wouldn't come amiss.'

When Miss Dolan had disappeared into the kitchen, the marshal turned to Forrest and Dowd. 'Like I just said, I reckon I'm about fit enough to ride. I ain't waitin' any longer to get after Ollinger and his bunch of no-good gunslicks. That's why I'm here. How do you two feel about joinin' me?'

'Are you plannin' on gettin' a posse together?' Forrest asked.

'Nope. I thought about it but even if anyone was available, they're still gonna be needed here. I've deputized someone to take care of things while I'm gone. Besides, I figure a small party can ride quicker and faster than a big one.'

'Why are you askin' us?' Forrest said.

'Didn't you say you had some business yourselves with Ollinger? Or did I just imagine that?'

Forrest and Dowd exchanged glances.

Forrest gave a sort of hollow laugh. 'Oh yes, we got business with him.'

Miss Dolan came back with the coffee. 'Here you are,' she said. She observed their grim faces. 'I guess you boys don't want disturbing', she said.

'It's fine,' the marshal replied. Miss Dolan poured and then left the room once more. They each took a drink.

'Best coffee in town,' the marshal said. 'Bar none, and I include the hotel. By the way, you two done a real good job helpin' to shore up the place. It won't be long till it's back in business.'

'Can't see you gettin' too many visitors,' Forrest replied.

'Oh, you'd be surprised.' The marshal grew suddenly grim and reflective. 'There's some more buryin's tomorrow,' he said. 'Once they're done, the town will start to get back on its feet again.' He looked across at Dowd. 'I just don't like buryin's,' he said.

As they were finishing their drinks, they could hear Miss Dolan moving about upstairs.

'She's a good woman,' the marshal said. 'I guess it's a sign I trusted you that I suggested you stay with her in the first place.'

'How long has she been in Mud Wagon Creek?'

'She came here a few years ago. She's a widow woman, even though folks call her Miss. Used to teach school once upon a time. Still helps out at the schoolhouse. Why do you ask?'

Forrest didn't know what to reply. He only knew that somehow the town had become linked with her in his mind, so that its cause was her cause.

'Well,' the marshal said, 'we ain't here to discuss Miss Dolan. Have you thought about what I was sayin'? About gettin' on the trail of Ollinger and his gang?'

'Three of us against all of them.'

'That's one more than you started out with,' Burden replied.

Forrest turned to Dowd. 'What do you say?' he asked.

'I say we go with the marshal,' Dowd replied.

'I'm of the same mind. Three's a good number. As far as I'm concerned, the quicker we find Ollinger the better it'll be.'

The marshal grinned. 'Good,' he said. 'Be ready to ride by noon tomorrow. Three against a crowd. I figure Ollinger's days are numbered.'

Next morning, having made their farewells to Miss Dolan, Forrest and Dowd joined Burden and rode out of town. Forrest felt strangely low. In the short time he had been at the boarding house, he had come to have a deep respect and admiration for the woman who had made them welcome. She had no need to have done so. She knew nothing about them. But she had shown them a degree of warmth over and above that required or expected of her professional role. On his part, Dowd too felt a strange rapport with the townsfolk they had been trying to help in their dire situation. Quite a few of the people he had met reminded him of the humble Mexican folk among

100

whom he had been living. At the recollection he felt again a stab of the old shame and guilt at having misled them for so long. His thoughts led him to remember the missing icon which was behind everything he was now involved in, as if it had some strange power to influence his actions. What had become of it? If this man Cushman didn't have it, who did? But Cushman probably did have it. He couldn't help feeling that Forrest had let Cushman off too lightly. Forrest was a strange man. He wasn't sure that he understood him. He needn't have got involved in any of this. He could simply have forgotten about the icon and ridden back to the Wine Glass. Life there must have been comparatively simple. The very fact that the owner of the Wine Glass had selected him for the trip to Mexico suggested he was trusted by Ringold.

Even after the lapse of time which had taken place since the attack on Mud Wagon Creek, the sign left by

Ollinger and his bunch of gunslicks was fairly easy for Forrest, Dowd and Burden to follow. The gunnies had gone in a generally north-westerly direction. Forrest was best at following the trail, but he was unable to say exactly how many riders Ollinger had at his command. It didn't make much difference. He already knew by bitter experience that there were a lot of them. As they rode, they found other traces of the passage of Ollinger and his gang in the shape of such detritus as empty cans and containers, a cast-off necktie and cigarette butts, but it was not till towards evening of the first day that they found evidence that the townsfolk's attempts at fighting back had not been entirely unsuccessful. For some time they had seen buzzards in the sky and, coming over the brow of a rise, they saw what had attracted them. Lying by the side of the trail were the festering remains of one of the gunmen. Forrest swung down from the saddle and, holding his bandanna over his face, he approached the corpse. Clouds of flies rose at his approach.

'Looks like he took a bullet in the chest,' he said. 'He got this far but they couldn't even take the time to bury him. There ain't much left to bury now.'

'He deserved everythin' he got,' Burden remarked. 'Let's hope he wasn't the only one.'

Forrest glanced towards Dowd. The erstwhile priest crossed himself and muttered a few words in a low tone. Forrest hesitated, looking back at the remains.

'Let's move on,' Burden said.

Putting aside any thoughts of burying what was left of the gunslick, Forrest climbed back into the saddle.

As they continued, Forrest was trying to think ahead to determine what Ollinger would be likely to do. If the evidence of Mud Wagon Creek was anything to go by, it was likely that he would seek the destruction of other towns. In addition, there were plenty of ranches he could attack. He tended to discount the notion of Ollinger continuing till he reached Oregon. Long before he got that far he would surely have aroused so much opposition that he would need to tone things down and maybe even return to the sanctuary of the Grand Springs ranch to lie low before eventually carrying on his trail of destruction. One thing concerned him, and that was that it wasn't just a question of them finding Ollinger. If he was right about the icon, at some stage the roles would be reversed and Ollinger would come looking for him.

Ollinger had got away with a lot of money from the bank robbery in Stinkweed and his standing was high with his men. There was little doubt in his mind that he could carry on that way for a long while; there were plenty of other targets. The one thing which would really set the seal on his career, however, would be if he could get his hands on that icon. Could he trust Cushman? Was Cushman right in his claim that Forrest had the icon? The way to find out was to find Forrest but there was no necessity for the whole outfit to be distracted in the search. He could send Cushman out with some of the others while he continued with the main body of the outlaws. It was a good plan. He had plenty of men riding for him and to detach a group of them would cause no difficulties. They would hardly be missed. He would put Rawlins in charge. In any case, if Cushman was to be believed, Forrest couldn't be too far away. If Cushman was playing him false, Rawlins would know how to deal with him. It was hard not to feel a real glow of satisfaction with the whole way things were moving. The world would regret ever having crossed swords with Oregon Boot Bass Ollinger. The sobriquet had become a kind of badge of honour. At first he had felt it was something of an insult, but not any longer. His thoughts made him glance down at his twisted foot. It made no difference whether the shackles were intended to injure and maim or not. It was irrelevant whether anyone else who had been forced to wear them had been affected in the same way. Those heavy iron contraptions had caused his injuries. He still suffered pain. Well, in return, the world that had persecuted him was going to feel pain: a lot of it. While Rawlins and Cushman were off after Forrest, he had a new target in mind for the rest of the gang: the stagecoach from Restitution to Sidgewick. It would pass quite close to Stinkweed. He had no way of knowing if the stage was carrying anything in the way of bullion, but it didn't matter. There would still be pickings to be had and the main thing was to keep the boys occupied.

4

Forrest opened his eyes. The night was dark and, staring up at the black spaces of the sky, for a moment he felt disoriented. Then he heard a faint sound and realized it must have been the same noise that had wakened him. He reached for his six-gun but did not immediately move. Instead he continued to listen but no further sounds reached his ears. He turned his head and then rolled on to his side. One bedroll was still occupied but the other was empty. He was about to rise when he thought he saw a shadowy shape glide across the open space by the fire and then a voice whispered close by: 'It's me, Dowd.'

Forrest was on his feet. 'What are you doin?' he said.

'Don't speak so loud. There's somethin' out there.'

Forrest had spoken in a whisper but he knew how far sounds carried on the open prairie. Without saying anything further, the two of them began to look around. Forrest's eyes had adjusted to the gloom but there was little he could detect. They began to move outwards from the camp, keeping low. A horse stamped but it was one of theirs. Crouching down, they waited and watched for anything that might emerge but they were disappointed. After what seemed a long time they slipped back and sat near the remains of the camp-fire. The marshal was still sleeping; they continued a silent vigil till the first rays of dawn began to flicker on the eastern horizon.

'Maybe we were wrong,' Dowd said.

'Maybe,' Forrest replied. 'When it's light I'm gonna take a look out there.'

Burden began to stir and they took it as a signal to start getting breakfast ready. Quickly, they built a fire and laid strips of bacon in the pan. Dowd filled the pot with water from their canteens

108

and set it to boil. When they had eaten they drank boiling hot coffee and as the earth began to lighten they talked about what had happened during the night.

'Sure you ain't both mistaken?' Burden said. 'I never heard nothin'.'

'Yeah, we could be. But it seems kinda strange that we both woke up.'

While Burden set about tidying up the camp and Dowd attended to the horses, Forrest strolled off to take a look around. Dowd had warned him to be careful but he had no worries that anybody would still be hanging about the vicinity. If there had been any threat, it would have come during the night. But he had a definite feeling that somebody or something had been there. As he walked he kept his eyes to the ground, searching for sign, but apart from some lizard trails and the faint indications of a sidewinder, there was nothing he could see. There was no surprise in that, but he felt disconcerted.

'Nothing?' Dowd inquired when he

came back. He shook his head.

'Looks like you just had bad dreams,' Burden said.

Forrest did not reply. He still wasn't willing to believe that both he and Dowd could have been mistaken.

Stepping into leather, they rode out, following the sign left by Ollinger and his gang. It had faded somewhat but it was still not difficult to follow. The morning passed and towards noon they were approaching a narrow stream bed with brush-covered banks on either side. Forrest was riding slightly ahead of the other two, observing the ground as they went. He rode down the slope and had just entered the stream when a shot rang out. Instantly he dug his spurs into the buckskin's flanks; the other two turned and began to ride down the river as a hail of fire burst from the brush on the opposite bank. Bullets tore up the surface of the water and Forrest's horse reared, toppling him from the saddle. Grabbing his rifle, he threw himself into the shallow water

110

and began to splash his way back across the stream. Dowd and Burden had dropped from their saddles and taken shelter behind some bushes a little lower downstream. One of their horses was lying near the water and the other had galloped away. Forrest reached a patch of tall reeds and crouched there, partly hidden by the over-hanging riverbank. Shots were ringing out and somebody was shouting but he couldn't make out who it was. Bringing his rifle to his shoulder, he began to fire at the bushes where the shots were coming from. Two things were obvious to him: there was a group of gunnies concealed among the bushes and they were almost certainly connected with Ollinger. One thing wasn't obvious, though, and that was how, with such an advantage they had failed to carry out their intentions. The first shot had given the game away. It had given them just enough time to take evasive measures. Maybe it had been meant as a warning shot. He didn't have time to give the matter a lot of consideration for the moment because bullets were hitting the water uncomfortably close to where he was hiding. He glanced down the river to where his companions had taken shelter. Shots were ringing out so Burden was certainly returning fire as well. He wondered for a moment if Dowd had any regrets about not carrying a weapon; they could certainly have done with an extra gun now. A fresh burst of fire rang out from the opposite bank; Forrest ducked below the surface of the water and as he emerged again he became aware that someone was firing from a position on the same side of the river a little further upstream. It wasn't Burden, so who could it be? His attention was caught by a flicker of movement among the bushes on the further side of the stream and for a moment he caught a glimpse of a figure. It was so brief that he had no time to take aim and fire, but there was something about the man he felt he definitely recognized. That distinctive buckskin jacket; could it have been Cushman? Cushman had said he wanted to get away from Ollinger but that was probably another lie. It wouldn't be surprising if he had decided to return to the Grand Springs ranch after all. If that was the case, then it meant that Ollinger was definitely out to get them and that he was not too far away.

Taking advantage of a lull in the firing, Forrest began to move away from where he had taken shelter in an effort to get nearer to where the stranger was positioned. Shots still rang out from that direction and from the comparative quiet which had descended, Forrest had a feeling that they had caused some consternation among the gunslicks, as if it was something they had not expected and were worried about. As far as Forrest could tell, there was only one person returning fire from that direction, but maybe the gunnies figured there could be more. He couldn't be certain himself. The stream took a slight curve and he reckoned he was probably out of sight of the gunslicks and protected from their fire, which had broken out again, but more sporadically. He contemplated getting out of the water and climbing the riverbank but decided against taking the risk. He felt chilled but at least the water was shallow, not coming any higher than his chest at its deepest point. Holding the rifle just above the surface, he waded on. He was out of sight of the patch of bushes where Burden and Dowd had taken cover but he could hear shots, which must have been coming from Burden's gun. There was a fresh burst of more concentrated fire from the opposite bank but none of it disturbed Forrest; he guessed it was aimed at Burden and Dowd rather than at him. Maybe the gunnies were unaware that he had shifted position. He was getting closer to whoever else was firing when he became aware that after the last salvo, the gunnies had gone quiet. A few more stray shots rang out and then there was comparative silence. He became conscious of the water lapping against the banks and then, after a short interlude, of a dull rumble which could only have been the sound of hoofbeats. It seemed as though the gunslicks had decided to call time on the battle, at least for the time being. He waited for a few more minutes and then began to drag himself out of the water. The bank was quite steep and slippery with mud at this point but after something of a struggle he succeeded in pulling himself on to dry ground where he lay panting with the effort before getting to his feet. He looked up the river towards where the shooting had come from and as he did so a voice called out.

'Mr Forrest, are you OK?'

Forrest couldn't see anybody but replied that he was unhurt.

'I'm coming out of cover,' the voice exclaimed.

There was a slight hiatus and then the bushes parted and a figure stepped out. Although he had only met him briefly, Forrest recognized Father Dowd's helper, Ignacio.

'Father Dowd,' Ignacio said. 'Is he safe too?'

'I don't know,' Forrest answered. 'Let's go and see.'

Together, they walked along the river-bank, taking care not to show themselves in case any of the gunslicks were still around. Shortly after they had passed the point at which Forrest had gone into the stream they saw the figures of Burden and Dowd walking towards them. Dowd's face registered incredulity when he recognized his housekeeper.

'Ignacio!' he gasped. 'What are you doing here? I thought you were in Caldera.'

There was blood flowing down Burden's cheek but he assured them that it was from nothing worse than a cut caused by flying shards of bark. For the first time, Forrest became aware of his own sodden condition. However, the sun was already doing a good job of drying him out.

'Let's leave the explanations till later,' he said. 'Those gunnies could be back any time. Let's round up the horses and get movin'.' He had to splash across the stream again to get his own horse. Dowd's horse had been killed but Burden's was OK.

'What do we do now?' Dowd said.

'It is not a problem,' Ignacio said. 'I have two horses, my own and a pack-horse. They are tethered in trees further down the river.'

As they walked back, Forrest turned to Ignacio. 'Tell me one thing,' he said. 'Was it you fired that first shot?'

'Yes, it was me,' Ignacio said. 'I could see no other way to warn you.'

'It was lucky you did,' Forrest replied. 'Without that warning, we'd all have been dead.'

Once they had organized the horses, they climbed into leather and rode away, carrying on in the same direction Forrest had been following before the attack. They crossed the stream and stopped briefly to examine where the outlaws had secreted themselves. There were three bodies among the bushes.

'Aren't we takin' a chance goin' in the same direction as those varmints?' Burden asked.

'It don't make any difference,' Forrest replied. 'If they want to come back and attack us again, they will do. In fact, they'll probably expect us to turn round and head in the opposite direction.'

'You figure it was Ollinger?' Burden said.

'Yeah, I'm sure it's him.' Forrest turned to Dowd. 'I caught a glimpse of one of them,' he added. 'I couldn't be certain, but I reckon it was Cushman.'

They rode on till the afternoon sun began to sink in the sky, looking out for a suitable camping ground. The ground was broken and rocky and it didn't take long till they found a suitable spot among some boulders backed by a stand of trees. A rivulet flowed down the slope of a low hill.

'This will do fine,' Forrest said.

They dismounted and set about

gathering material for a fire which they laid in a space between some rocks that gave them cover but also allowed a clear and uninterrupted view of the terrain. When everything had been tended to and they had relieved their hunger with a good meal of bacon, beans and coffee, Forrest handed round his pouch of Bull Durham. They built smokes.

'Well,' Forrest said, addressing his remarks to Ignacio, 'I reckon we're all curious to know how you happened along.'

Ignacio looked at them a little shamefacedly. He felt guilty about having taken the icon and wasn't sure how to go about explaining his actions so as to put them in the best possible light. He needn't have worried too much, though, because Dowd, especially, was so relieved that Ignacio had the icon that the right and wrongs of the matter were of no concern.

'Hell,' Forrest said when he had finished, 'so it was you had the icon all along. I was just about convinced

Cushman had lied to me and he had it.'

'Where is it now, Ignacio?' Dowd said.

'Do not worry. It is safe in my saddle-bags.'

Dowd didn't look happy. 'Perhaps you'd better check,' he said.

Ignacio got to his feet and walked over to where the horses were grazing. In a few moments he was back with a bundle in his hand. 'Here it is. Take good care of it,' he said.

Dowd unwrapped the bundle. As Ignacio had said, the icon was safe inside. Gently, he held it up to the firelight for the others to see. Ignacio crossed himself and muttered a prayer beneath his breath.

'It is a lovely thing,' Dowd said, 'but I still can't understand why Ollinger takes such an interest in it.'

'Yeah, that's what I can't figure out,' Forrest said.

He looked closely at the icon before passing it on to Burden. Ignacio looked uncomfortable again and Forrest assumed it was because he was concerned about the way they were handling the icon.

'It is not that,' Ignacio said when Forrest assured him that they would take care of the precious object. 'It's that I think I might have an idea about why Ollinger wants the icon.' Forrest and Dowd looked at him with renewed interest.

'I don't know if you have heard anything of the rumours surrounding the icon,' Ignacio said, addressing the priest. Dowd shook his head.

'No, I have not heard of any rumours.'

'It may be nothing,' Ignacio said. 'It may be just a story.'

'Go ahead and say what you know,' Dowd said. 'Then we can be the judge of the matter.'

'Well,' Ignacio continued, 'the icon of the Virgin of the Sign is said to be one of two which were brought here a long time ago.'

'I knew something of that,' Dowd interjected.

'The other picture is said to be equally beautiful but together they make a whole. You have, of course, seen the writing on the back.'

'Yes,' Dowd said.

Burden turned the icon over and read out the single word *Innere*.

'The word is German and means *interior*,' Dowd commented.

'Don't seem to make a lot of sense,' Forrest replied.

Ignacio's eyes flickered from one to the other. 'As I said, the icon is one of two. People say that there is something written on the back of the other one and if the two are ever brought together, it will spell out the location of a place where much treasure is to be found. I believe that Ollinger may have the other one.'

'A lot of hogwash, I would think,' Burden said. 'But what do I know? I hadn't even heard any of this before now.'

'It may be hogwash,' Forrest said. 'But it would sure explain why Ollinger is so keen to get his hands on the icon. The prospect of a big horde of loot would be just the thing to lure him on.'

Dowd seemed to be musing over the writing on the back of the icon. '*Interior*,' he repeated. 'There doesn't seem to be much in that one word. I've seen it many times and not thought about it twice.'

'It wouldn't matter whether it means anything or not,' Forrest said. 'As long as Ollinger believes there is some kind of message involved, he won't rest till he's got that icon in his hands.' He turned his attention back to Ignacio. 'Tell me,' he said, 'was that you last night prowling about near our camp? Both Father Dowd and myself were woken up by something.'

'Yes, it must have been me. I saw your camp-fire and tried to get close to see who it was. I couldn't get near enough to be certain it was you. Today, when I saw those gunslicks, I figured they were plannin' to dry-gulch someone. I hid in the bushes. I wasn't sure whether they were aimin' for you or somebody else. It was too late to warn you. When I saw you ride into the water, I couldn't think of anything to do but fire a shot.'

'It worked,' Burden said. 'And not a second too soon.'

'Did you see how many of them there were?' Forrest inquired.

'Not exactly,' Ignacio replied. 'About eight, I reckon.'

'Then Ollinger must have split his forces,' Forrest mused. 'There was a lot more than that involved in burning down Mud Wagon Creek.'

'What do you reckon he'll do next?' Burden asked.

'Who knows? But he'll be plannin' somethin'.'

For a while they lapsed into silence, finishing off the coffee and smoking their cigarettes. Forrest was meditating on what Ignacio had told them.

'Sooner or later Ollinger is goin' to head back to the Grand Springs,' he said. 'Probably after he's done another job or two and wants to lie low for a time. That might be the time we catch up with him.'

124

'It's worth keepin' in mind,' Burden said.

'Yeah, but I'm thinkin' of somethin' else,' Forrest replied. 'Until that time, the Grand Springs will be pretty quiet. He'll have left men behind to look after the place but there probably won't be too many of 'em. The ones that have been left ain't likely to be among his best gunslingers.'

'You got somethin' in mind,' Burden said. It was a statement rather than a question.

'I might be all wrong about this,' Forrest said, 'but it seems to me that if Ollinger is in possession of that other icon Ignacio was talkin' about, then it's likely he keeps it at the ranch.'

'That seems reasonable,' Father Dowd said. 'But how does that concern us?'

'A lot of Ollinger's thinkin' seems to revolve around those icons. He figures that if he can bring the two icons together, he'll have the clue to this horde of treasure. If there's any truth in the rumour, I dread to think what he might get up to with that sort of money behind him. So why don't we steal a march on him and see if we can lay our hands on that other icon, the one he apparently has?' The others thought about his proposition.

'I see what you're gettin' at,' Burden replied. 'And I got to say, it's beginnin' to make sense to me.'

Father Dowd looked less convinced. 'You might have a point,' he said, 'but, apart from other considerations, how do you propose to get hold of the icon?'

'Like we just agreed, the number of Ollinger's men remainin' at the ranch is likely to be down to a minimum. I figure we could ride right on in there without bein' detected. Once we get to the ranch house, we sneak in and do a little search.'

'That would amount to burglary,' Dowd commented.

Forrest gave him a quizzical look. 'I reckon, in view of what's been happenin', that's the least of it,' he said.

The beginnings of a smile lifted the corners of the priest's mouth. 'Yes, I see what you mean,' he replied.

Burden burst into a laugh. 'You sure ain't like most other people I can think of,' he said to Dowd. 'Hell, I don't know anyone else who would have rode into that ambush without a gun. What would you have done if I hadn't had mine?'

Dowd did not reply, deciding to treat it as a rhetorical question.

'So what do you say?' Forrest continued. 'Do we head for the Grand Springs ranch?' They exchanged glances.

'I'm for it,' Burden said.

'I'll go along with what you decide,' Dowd answered.

Forrest turned towards Ignacio. 'What about you?' he said. 'You get a say in this as well.'

Ignacio glanced at Dowd who acknowledged his look with a barely perceptible nod. 'I came all this way to be with you,' he said.

'OK, then it's decided,' Forrest concluded. 'For now, I guess we'd better arrange guard duties. I don't figure those gunnies are gonna return tonight, but I guess we can't afford to take any chances.'

Once they had worked out their turn at taking guard, they settled down for the night, Dowd taking the first watch. He moved to the front of the camp and settled himself behind a rock. The night was strangely luminous and he could see for a long distance ahead of him. There was no danger of him falling asleep on the job because his head was filled with conflicting ideas and impressions. Along with the sense of guilt which had come to haunt him and his mixed views about their current predicament, he found himself questioning his decision not to carry a gun. Burden's comments had touched a nerve. Did he have any right to rely on other people when it came to a shoot-out like they had experienced earlier? Was he not putting the lives of other people in greater jeopardy? And what would he have done if he had been there when Ollinger attacked the township of Mud Wagon Creek, faced perhaps with the choice of defending a hapless citizen against one of Ollinger's gunnies? Even more to the point, what would he do if they were attacked tonight and he had to do something to defend the others? As often happened, he found himself turning to prayer. He reached into his pocket and, drawing out the chain of beads, began to count his rosary.

It was not long past the middle of another night when they approached the Grand Springs ranch. They knew they were on Ollinger's property when they rode under a huge gallows-like structure which marked the entrance to his range. Peering through the darkness, Dowd read the sign it carried: *Grand Springs — Grubbin' and Sharpin' a Speciality.*

'Enigmatic,' he said. 'What's it supposed to mean?'

'A grub is a mark made by cuttin' a cow's entire ear off close to the head,' Forrest replied, 'only in this case I don't think it's referrin' to cattle.'

'Very welcomin',' Burden said. 'I hope any visitors would understand the reference.'

They spurred their horses on, keeping their eyes open for indications of activity. Since they could see very little, however, apart from the occasional dim shapes of cattle, it was unlikely that anyone would be able to see them. Their horses' hoofs beat a muffled rhythm and there was an occasional creak of leather but otherwise they were silent. Once they had entered the Grand Springs range, Father Dowd expected them to arrive fairly soon at the ranch house, but instead they seemed to carry on for mile after mile. Forrest knew how extensive Ollinger's property was. It would be even bigger if Ollinger had his way and swallowed up other ranches in the region. Just as Father Dowd was beginning to think they would never get there, the long black shape of Ollinger's ranch house loomed up like a natural barrier.

'Better get down and leave the horses here,' Forrest said.

They dismounted and tethered their mounts. It had already been arranged that Ignacio would stay with them while the others proceeded to the ranch house.

'You sure you're OK with that?' Forrest said.

'Yes. Good luck.'

Ignacio was more relaxed than Forrest imagined. He had the icon to give him support. Forrest looked at the others. 'You know what you have to do?' he said. They nodded their assent. 'All right, let's get movin'.'

They started forward towards the lowering bulk of the ranch house. The place was entirely shrouded in darkness. There were no lights in any of the windows and the place gave every indication of being deserted. Behind and to the right of it stood another building which Forrest guessed was probably the bunkhouse. He was more concerned about this than he was about

131

the main building. Ollinger would have left some men behind to run the ranch in his absence and most of them must be there. He could only hope and pray that they were all asleep. Somewhere beyond the bunkhouse they could hear the occasional stamp and snicker of horses. They came through the open area of the yard and mounted the veranda steps. The difficult part was just about to begin.

Forrest tested the door but as he expected, it was locked. He moved round to the nearest window and attempted to raise the sash but to no avail. He tried the other windows without any luck. 'OK,' he whispered. 'We'll try the back.'

Silently, they crept along the veranda past the corner of the building away from the bunkhouse. A board creaked under Dowd's foot and they froze. The sound seemed excessively loud in the silence of the night. After a few moments they continued. There were several windows along the side of the house and Forrest tried them, with the same results. They came round to the rear of the building. In front of them but still some distance away they could make out the corrals. The sound of the horses was louder and Forrest signalled to the others to take care not to spook them. There were a similar number of windows at the back but they were all tight closed. Forrest was not too concerned. He would have been surprised if any of them had been ajar.

'OK,' he said. 'We're gonna have to break the glass.'

'I don't like this,' Dowd said.

'Do you think we do?' Forrest replied.

'What about the noise?' Burden whispered.

'It can't be helped.'

'Hold on a minute,' Burden replied. 'I think I got a better idea. Let's return to the front.'

When they had retraced their steps, Burden signalled for the others to keep watch and, producing a wire from his pocket, began to fumble with the lock. After trying for some time to spring it he stopped, put the wire back in his pocket, and produced another one. Again he began to manoeuvre the wire and just when it seemed his efforts would prove equally fruitless, something clicked. Burden turned to the others and they could just make out a thin smile on his face. 'Comes of dealin' with law-breakers,' he said. 'You get to pick up a few tricks of the trade.'

He pushed gently on the door and it opened. Like shades of the night they slipped through into the ranch house. Burden immediately bumped into something and there was a clattering noise. They halted in their tracks, waiting to see if there would be any response. Nothing happened and as they waited their eyes gradually adjusted to the dark.

'Seems like we're OK,' Forrest whispered. 'But be careful. We can't afford to take any risks.' Burden had knocked over a small table, which he proceeded to set aright. 'Chances are that the icon will be somewhere in the main room if it's anywhere,' Forrest said. He turned to Burden. 'Me and Dowd will concentrate on here if you start on the rest of the house.'

Burden nodded and very carefully began to pick his way towards a staircase which disappeared into blackness over their heads.

'You take that side, I'll take this,' Forrest said.

Dowd moved away and Forrest began to look closely at various items of furniture, starting with a large escritoire which stood near a curtained window. He pulled the drawers but they were all locked. He was thinking all the while of the most likely place for the icon to be kept. As he crept about the room, he almost forgot the presence of the priest until a small collision in the darkness reminded him of it. His thoughts kept returning to the escritoire. A piece of furniture like that seemed the likeliest place to find it. The presence of the escritoire made him wonder if Ollinger might have a private study where he conducted business. There was a door at the back of the room but when he placed his fingers on the knob and pushed he was disappointed. It, too, was locked. As he turned back he was struck by a thought. Maybe Ollinger kept his valuables in a safe. The moment the idea crossed his mind it seemed obvious. He looked up at the walls. There were a number of paintings as well as mirrors and a clock. Curiously, it was only when he saw it that he became conscious of its quiet steady tick. There didn't seem to be anything resembling a safe. He was standing considering the matter when Dowd bumped into him again.

'I don't think this is a good idea,' Dowd said. 'If Ollinger has an icon, it could be anywhere.'

'I'm beginnin' to think you're right,' Forrest said. He was about to suggest they take a final look when there was a loud click and before they could work out what had caused it the door of the room was flung open. They heard a rush of feet as dim shapes loomed up out of the darkness. Before they could react they had been seized and their arms pinioned. A lamp was lit and they were faced by a man with a gun in his hand.

'Take their weapons,' he said. Forrest's six-gun was deftly removed.

'This one ain't carryin' a gun,' someone replied. Forrest turned his head. Each of them was being held by two men.

'Who are you?' the man with the gun said. 'And what are you doin' here?'

Despite his predicament, Forrest's eyes observed that one of the paintings on the wall hung slightly loose.

'Start talkin',' the man said.

Forrest's eyes dropped to their questioner. If he had ever seen a more low-down mean desperado than this one, he couldn't remember where or when. He had little doubt that, though he could not see much of them, his colleagues were of the same stamp. He realized that they could expect no mercy. As if to confirm the impression, when Forrest and Dowd remained silent, the man stepped forward and punched Dowd hard in the stomach.

'I said, start talkin',' the man repeated.

Dowd would have fallen if he hadn't been supported. Forrest jerked forward in an attempt to throw off his own captors but they had his arms held as if in a vice.

'Looks like we're gonna have to try a little more persuasion,' the leader said.

There was an answering chuckle but the laughter was caught short when a voice called out of the shadows: 'Drop your gun or die!'

There was no mistaking the startled look on the gunman's features. The voice seemed to be disembodied. Ignoring its command, he spun round, bent over with his arm outstretched in the shooting position. By way of reply there came a shattering explosion from the direction of the stairway and the man went reeling back, clutching at his arm and dropping his gun. The grip on Forrest slackened and he burst free, turning as he did so to aim a blow at one of the men behind him. The man staggered and crashed into the escritoire. The other two had released their hold on Dowd who slumped forward on to his knees.

'Don't make another move,' the voice commanded, 'or I fire again.'

Forrest looked across the room. He had forgotten about Burden who now appeared at the foot of the stairs.

'Take their guns,' he said to Forrest. When he had done so, Forrest turned to Dowd and helped him to his feet.

'There's a cupboard upstairs,' Burden said. 'I suggest we lock 'em in and then get out of here. Somebody might have heard that gunshot.'

'Sounds like a good idea,' Forrest replied. He turned to Dowd. 'You sure you're gonna be OK.'

'Sure, I'll be fine,' Dowd said.

'All right,' Forrest said to the five

139

gunnies, 'you heard the man.'

There was some reluctance on their part but they had little choice. Their leader had been hit in the arm and he was in no condition to offer resistance. Alternatively cursing and groaning, he began to mount the stairs when Forrest had a second thought.

'Hold it just a minute,' he said. 'Keep them covered while I take a look at something.'

He quickly moved across the room to the picture. He felt around it and then tugged at the spot where it seemed to be hanging slightly loose from the wall. The picture swung back to reveal a safe. Forrest tried to open it but it was locked. Taking his gun, he fired two shots at the lock. The noise was deafening but when he tried again, the door opened. He reached inside. There were rolls of money and some items of jewellery but he ignored them in favour of a small parcel wrapped in a cloth. Quickly he undid the bundle; inside was the icon.

'I think we got what we came for,' he said.

Without wasting any more time, they ushered the gunslicks up the stairs and pushed them into the cupboard. It was quite spacious but it was still an uncomfortable fit. There was no key and Forrest was about to suggest they pile up furniture to keep the door closed when Burden produced his wire.

'You didn't give me a chance to see if it would have worked on that safe,' he said. It took a matter of moments for him to lock the door on the gunnies.

'You can't leave us in here!' a voice exclaimed.

Ignoring the pleas of the trapped men, they rushed down the stairs. Burden extinguished the lamp and then, slamming the door behind them, they began to run to their horses. Ignacio was still there.

'I heard a shot,' he said. 'I didn't know what to do.'

'You did right to stay with the horses,' Forrest said.

'We were damn lucky no one else was around,' Burden gasped as they swung into leather. 'Things could have got really unpleasant if some others had been in the bunkhouse and heard the shootin'.'

'I don't think it'll be too long till those varmints bust out of there,' Forrest replied. 'Let's put some distance between them and us.'

He reached in his pocket to check that the icon was safe and then they started to ride. They kept going for some time, loping along at a steady pace. The first glimmerings of dawn were beginning to lighten the horizon when they drew to a halt in the shelter of some rocks and bushes.

'This will do fine,' Forrest said. 'I don't know about you, but I reckon I'm about ready to call it a night.'

His curiosity about the icon had been growing as they rode. What were its secrets? What words were written on the back?

They got down and began to make

camp. When they had gathered the materials for a fire and were about to start it alight, Ignacio suddenly gestured for them to be quiet. They listened carefully. From the direction of the ranch they could discern the sound of galloping hoofs.

'Hell, looks like those gunnies got out quicker than we thought,' Forrest said.

'Why worry,' Burden said. 'There were only five of 'em.'

'There's more than five of 'em now,' Ignacio said.

'Are you sure? How can you tell?'

'I can tell,' Ignacio answered.

'I say we wait and settle it this time,' Burden replied. They looked towards Forrest.

'We got a good spot here,' Forrest said, 'and I'm kinda tired of those varmints. I agree with Burden.'

Father Dowd hadn't spoken. The others turned towards him. Burden was expecting the priest to raise objections. Dowd looked slowly from one to the other.

'Are you OK about this?' he addressed Ignacio.

143

Ignacio looked a little sheepish. 'I think I stay,' he replied.

Father Dowd continued to look at his housekeeper and then a smile slowly spread across his features. 'You have always been a good man,' he said. 'Now I see that you are a brave man.' He turned to Forrest. 'I think we both stay,' he said.

Forrest grinned. 'That's good. Then we are all agreed. Find some place to take cover and keep out of the way when the bullets fly.'

'No,' Father Dowd said. Forrest and Burden gave him a puzzled look.

'I will not 'keep out of the way', as you say. I will fight alongside the rest of you.' The others still did not understand.

'Give me a gun,' Father Dowd said. 'It is not right that I let others fight while I do not. At this moment I see that there are times when a man must take his stand. Maybe I'll think different tomorrow.'

Forrest opened his mouth to reply

but then closed it again. Instead of speaking he stepped to his horse and pulled a rifle from its scabbard. Moving back, he threw it to the priest. 'Guess you know how to use a Winchester,' he said.

Father Dowd's smile widened. 'Yeah, guess I do,' he replied.

Without further delay they took cover. The rhythmic beat of hoofs had grown loud and presently through the gathering light the riders appeared. Ignacio was right about there being more of them. As they drew close Forrest tried to see whether he recognized any of them but he couldn't be sure. Certainly the leader of the men who had surprised them was not there; presumably he had been left behind to nurse his wound. They were still out of shooting range when they drew to a stop. Forrest had no doubt in his mind that the gunnies would know exactly where they were concealed. Their tracks were new and sufficiently obvious for them to have been able to follow, even in the gloom. Now the riders began to dismount and take up positions, continuing to keep out of range. They made a good job of concealing themselves; only once did Forrest see a flicker of movement during the long hiatus which followed. Forrest glanced across at the others. They were all concentrating on what was happening. The minutes ticked by. It seemed that the outlaws were in no hurry. They were playing a waiting game, presumably hoping to unnerve their opponents. That was OK with Forrest. A heavy silence seemed to hang over the scene till a bird began to chatter somewhere. The sun emerged and began its slow climb across the sky, bathing the prairie in a crystal glow. Forrest was content to let the outlaws make the first move. Maybe it would come in the form of some ultimatum. Suddenly he heard a scraping sound from somewhere above and behind him. In an instant he had swung round and squeezed the trigger of his gun. In that brief moment he had seen a figure partly concealed by a rock. He didn't know how it had happened, but some of the outlaws had succeeded in outflanking them. His shot ricocheted from the rock and went whining overhead.

'Watch out!' he shouted, but the others were already alert to the danger and had changed their positions to take account of the new situation. Forrest rolled away as shots rang out behind them, followed instantly by a fusillade of gunfire from the gunnies out in front. They had got closer but most of their shooting was wild. It was the outlaws who had succeeded in getting behind them that were a priority. They needed to be dealt with quickly.

Apart from the one person he had glimpsed, Forrest had no idea how many of them there were. Signalling to Burden to keep him covered, he sprang to his feet and darted for some bushes to his rear. Burden's rifle slammed. Bullets tore up the ground near his feet but he made it to the bushes and threw himself into cover. The battle he had just left was raging but he continued moving away from it, taking care to remain concealed. He reached the rising ground where he figured the outlaws had managed to secrete themselves. There were some big boulders and, as he crept forward, a figure suddenly appeared from behind one. The man's gun spoke but Forrest's gun was quicker and the outlaw slumped to the ground as splinters of rock showered from the rock next to where Forrest was standing. Out of the corner of his eye he saw movement above him and, swinging his rifle up, he fired again. The man was standing on top of a pinnacle of rock; he flung up his arms, arched forward and somersaulted to the ground beneath. It was Forrest's last bullet and he was about to put the rifle aside and draw his six-guns when there was a warning shout from somewhere behind him. Instinctively he looked up and saw another gunnie just ahead of him with his rifle raised. Before the man could squeeze the trigger there was a shot from behind them both and Forrest spun round to see Dowd with a smoking rifle in his hands. He heard a grunt and turned back as the gunnie staggered backwards and fell to the ground, dropping his rifle as he did so. Before Forrest could do or say anything, he heard the sound of someone running. He started in pursuit but when he reached a more open space and looked around, there was no sign of the runner. He waited for a few moments with his gun in his hand before the sound of hoofs told him that whoever the man was, he had got away. The sounds of gunfire had dwindled and then he heard Burden's voice calling out. He turned and began to make his way back towards his original position. Dowd was still standing where he had seen him.

'Thanks,' Forrest said. 'I didn't spot him. He would have killed me.'

Dowd's face was white and drawn. He didn't reply.

'Come on,' Forrest said. 'Let's get back to the others.'

They were about to push their way through the bushes when there was another shout from Burden. 'Forrest! Are you OK?'

'I'm all right,' he shouted back, but his voice was drowned by an eruption of gunfire followed by a sudden silence. Signalling to Dowd to follow him, Forrest pushed his way through the bushes. As he emerged he was surprised to see Burden and Ignacio standing up and embracing one another.

'Get down, you fools!' Forrest shouted but they just turned and laughed.

'Listen!' Burden said.

Forrest paused and after a few moments the silence was broken by the sounds of hoofbeats which soon began to fade.

'They've had enough,' Burden said. 'That's the rest ridin' off.'

'How about you?' Ignacio said. 'What happened?'

'Some of 'em got round behind us,'

Forrest said. 'One got away.'

Dowd had emerged from cover and stood slightly apart. Forrest glanced at him but something told him it might be best to let the priest react in his own way. Instead he addressed the others. 'That's twice we've beat off a bunch of the varmints,' he said. 'Let's hope our luck holds for the next time.'

5

The town of Stinkweed hadn't suffered as badly as Mud Wagon Creek at the hands of Ollinger and his gang, but the damage was serious enough. Several innocent citizens had been killed and the townsfolk were deeply affected by what had happened to them and to Mr Meeker. A long-term resident and prominent citizen of the town, he had been behind much of its development in his role as head of the bank. A large number of the townsfolk had got a start in business through his financial encouragement and when times were bad, a lot of them owed it to him that they had pulled through. He had been a good friend to many of them, not least to Marshal Kip Arnold. Meeker and Arnold had known each other for a long time. To add to his grief and his anger, Arnold felt particularly bitter that he had been fooled by the outlaws' diversion long enough for the bank robbers to make a clean getaway. However, he had no intention of letting them escape. Given the fact that feelings were running high among the townsfolk, it didn't take too long for him to form a posse despite the realization that they would be up against a substantial number of desperados. If they had known anything about Oregon Boot Bass Ollinger it might have made a difference to some, but not to Arnold. He was an experienced lawman whose reputation was such that he could normally rely on buffaloing a miscreant rather than resorting to gunplay. But when the occasion called for it, he knew how to throw lead.

He was in his office making some final arrangements about the posse when the door flew open and a young boy ran in. 'Marshal Arnold! Marshal Arnold!' he shouted breathlessly. 'Someone's attacked the stage.'

He leaped to his feet and slammed out the door in the boy's wake. As he approached the stagecoach depot he could see a number of people milling about. The depot manager met him as he ran up. 'In here,' he said.

Arnold entered the building. Lying on a makeshift bed was the stagecoach driver. The doctor had just removed a bullet from his arm. He looked up groggily at the marshal's entrance.

'Can you talk?' Arnold said.

The man grimaced. 'Yeah. There was a whole bunch of 'em. They killed the messenger and beat up a couple of the passengers.'

'Where did this take place?' Arnold said.

'About fifteen miles out of town. We picked up some passengers at Restitution and left early this mornin'.'

Arnold did a quick calculation. There was no doubt in his mind that the same gang which had robbed the bank and killed Meeker was responsible. The fact that they had committed both atrocities was symptomatic of their overweening confidence. He had expected a long, hard ride in pursuit of them, but it seemed that wasn't to be the case. They were still in the vicinity, probably not more than twenty or thirty miles away. He turned to the station manager. 'Anything taken?' he snapped.

'Nothin' except some of the passengers' belongin's. That's what I don't understand. The stage wasn't carryin' anything of any particular value.'

'I guess those varmints are hell-raisin' for fun,' Arnold replied.

After questioning the passengers, he walked quickly back to his office and swung into the saddle of the big Appaloosa which was standing at the hitch rack outside. He rode past the depot, which was still the scene of animated activity and started down the trail to Restitution, following the tracks of the stagecoach. It was easy to locate the scene of the attack. He jumped down and examined the ground. There must have been about ten horsemen; it confirmed Arnold's supposition that he was faced with a big gang of gunnies, especially, as in all likelihood, it was a different bunch of them from the one that had robbed the bank. He got back into leather and rode on, following the trail left by the gang for another couple of miles or so when the ground grew stonier and it was harder to make out their sign. At least he had a good idea of the direction they had taken. It was time to get back to Stinkwood and gather the posse together.

Arnold was right. Oregon Boot Bass Ollinger wasn't concerned about a posse getting on his trail. If it happened, it was just one of the hazards of the job and he could deal with it. The prospect was of no importance to him. The outlaw leader was in a bad mood for other reasons. First of all Rawlins and Cushman had returned with their tails between their legs, having failed to deal with Forrest. If that wasn't enough, he had just got word of the burglary at the Grand Springs. That was the thing which really concerned him. The rider who had brought him the news wasn't able to say just exactly what had been taken, but it was pretty clear to Ollinger that it must have included the icon. If so, it was a serious matter and he needed to think things out. Was that *hombre* Forrest involved? And just exactly what was his role in all this? The more he thought about it, the more clear it seemed that whoever else had taken part in the burglary, Forrest was the moving force. It followed that Forrest must be in possession of the other icon. What motive could he have for breaking into the ranch house other than to match up the two icons and be in possession of the secret location of the treasure? It was incumbent now to catch up with Forrest. It was a bad situation, but he could see a possible glimmer of light. If Forrest was in possession of both icons, it would make things a lot easier once he tracked him down. But where was Forrest? It shouldn't be too difficult to find him.

He was weighing up the options when another thought struck him with a powerful force. Without further delay, he sent for Cushman.

'I'm real sorry,' Cushman began, about to repeat what he had already said to Ollinger. 'Someone warned Forrest and — '

'Shut up!' Ollinger ordered. 'I ain't interested in that now. I want you to tell me again just what happened at the Wine Glass R to put you on the track of this man Forrest in the first place.'

Cushman looked confused.

'Go on, get on with it.'

'I already told you — '

Cushman didn't get any further because Ollinger had seized him by the collar of his shirt and pressed the muzzle of a revolver against his forehead.

'Tell me again. And you'd better make it the truth.' He slammed Cushman hard against a rock. Cushman fell, hitting his head. He got back to his feet, blood streaming from a jagged cut to his cheek. 'I'm listenin',' Ollinger said.

'I did exactly what you told me. I got a job at the Wine Glass. I listened out. I talked to people. I hung about the ranch house but it didn't seem like I was goin' to find anything till I struck lucky and overheard Ringold tellin' Forrest to ride down to Mexico and get that icon. As soon as I heard about it I set off for Mexico so I could get there before Forrest.'

'And what happened when you got there?'

'I traced the icon to a church in a place called Caldera. I met the priest. I recognized him. He was somebody once rode with us in the old days, Dowd — '

'Dowd?' Ollinger interrupted. 'I don't remember the name.'

'There were a lot of people came and went. He wasn't important.'

'And what happened to the icon?' Ollinger said.

'Like I said, this man Forrest beat me to it.'

'I'm still not convinced you didn't take it yourself. If I were to find out — '

'I swear I ain't lyin'. It was Forrest who took it.'

Ollinger glanced disdainfully at the grovelling figure in front of him. He didn't know how much was the truth and how much was a lie. The one thing he was sure about was that Cushman had let him down, and more than once. He'd had his chance. Slowly he raised the six-gun and pointed it at Cushman's head.

'Please, Mr Ollinger. You got to believe — '

Cushman didn't get any further. There were two loud explosions as Ollinger squeezed the trigger. One bullet smashed into Cushman's head and the other slammed into his chest. For a brief moment his eyes alone continued to plead with Ollinger before they closed for ever. Ollinger turned away. His brief conversation with Cushman had convinced him that Forrest was not working alone. He was still acting on behalf of Ringold. The Wine Glass was the likeliest place to find Forrest. It was time to deal with Forrest and the Wine Glass, both.

Father Dowd had remained silent

and withdrawn since the shoot-out at the Grand Springs. He had insisted on burying the outlaws who had been killed; it had taken them some time but it had been done. By the time it was finished the day had advanced considerably. They climbed into leather and at last shook off the dust of the Grand Springs. They rode on, Forrest and Burden taking the lead with Father Dowd and Ignacio bringing up the rear, till darkness descended and they made camp. It was only when they had eaten and made themselves comfortable that Forrest thought again about the icon. They had all been caught up in events until then. As he looked across the flickering firelight at the others, he wondered if the same thing was on their minds when his unspoken thought was answered by Burden.

'Well,' he said, 'I reckon that thing we took's caused enough trouble already. Maybe now's the time we had a look at it.'

'That's what I was thinkin',' Forrest

replied. 'We gone through a lot to bring those two icons together. Let's see if there's any truth in that story of Ignacio's.'

'It is something I have heard, nothing more,' Ignacio replied. 'In all likelihood it is just an idle tale.'

'There's only one way to find out,' Burden said.

Forrest turned to Father Dowd. He had an odd feeling that the priest's agreement was somehow necessary, as if in some way they needed his approval before they went any further.

'That all right with you, Father?' he said, unconscious of addressing the priest by that title. Father Dowd seemed to weigh the matter for a few moments.

'I think we owe it to ourselves,' he replied.

Forrest dug in his pocket and produced the icon they had taken from Ollinger's ranch house. With a glance at Father Dowd, Ignacio got to his feet, walked to the horses, and took the icon of the Virgin of the Sign out of his saddle-bags. Without thinking, they both handed them to Father Dowd who carefully began to unwrap them. When he had done so he laid them side by side on his blanket. It was the first time Burden had seen either of them and the first time the others had seen the companion piece to the Virgin of the Sign. The second icon was slightly smaller and portrayed the Virgin in a different way, cradling the child Christ in her left arm while pointing to him with her right.

'The Virgin here is the *Hodegetria*,' Father Dowd said, 'she who shows the way because she points to Christ.'

Ignacio had fallen to his knees and all four of them looked with rapt attention at the two representations in the pulsating glow of the firelight. Forrest felt moved in the same way he had when Father Dowd first showed him the icon of the Sign back in Caldera. It was Father Dowd himself who eventually reminded them of their purpose in unwrapping the icons.

'Ignacio told us the legend said that the clue to the treasure lay in the writing on the back of the icons, so shall we take a look?' Very gently, he turned the icons over. 'We know already that the word on the back of the *Orans* is *Innere* which means *interior*. What does it say on the back of the other?'

They peered closely. There was indeed something written on the back of the icon but they couldn't make out what it was. Father Dowd carefully picked it up and held it close to his face.

'What does it say?' Burden asked.

'It says *Berg*,' he replied. 'That means *mountain*.' His words were met with a puzzled silence until Burden spoke again.

'*Interior mountain*. What is that supposed to mean?'

'It sure don't make a lot of sense to me,' Forrest said. 'Is there a place called *Interior Mountain*? If there is, it could be anywhere.'

They looked at Father Dowd. Slowly

his face, which had been lined with stress and anxiety, seemed to relax and a gentle smile replaced his former grim expression.

'There is a place called *Interior Mountain*,' he said, 'but it is not anywhere outside. Just as it says, it is within.'

Forrest and Burden exchanged glances. 'I don't think I get you,' Burden said.

'The mountain is where God speaks. It was on Sinai where God delivered the Law to Moses. It was on a mountain where Christ pronounced the Beatitudes. So the mountain is where God speaks to you in the innermost part of your being.'

'So there ain't no clue to any treasure?' Burden replied. There was silence for a few moments before Forrest spoke.

'It's kinda funny when you think about it,' he said, 'people spendin' so much time and effort for nothin', for what turns out to be just some crazy kind of pipe-dream.'

Father Dowd was still smiling. 'Depends which way you look at it,' he said, 'on what kind of treasure you're seeking. Depends where your treasure is.'

'I still don't get it,' Burden repeated.

'Better pack these two icons away for now,' Forrest said. 'Then we gotta decide what we do next.'

Father Dowd wrapped up the two icons and gave them both to Ignacio. 'Here,' he said. 'You can be their protector now.'

Ignacio took them reverently in his hands and then walked back to the horses where he placed them carefully in his saddle-bags.

'That still leaves the problem of Ollinger,' Forrest said. 'With or without those icons, he needs to be stopped.'

'That's what I come for,' Burden said. 'Now that's somethin' I do understand.'

'Here's what I reckon,' Forrest said. 'Sooner or later Ollinger's goin' to know what happened at his ranch. He's no fool. He'll realize that the icon's been taken.'

'What do you figure he'll do?'

Forrest chuckled softly. 'He sure ain't gonna be pleased,' he said.

'You reckon it'll make him even more determined to find us?'

'Yes, but I also reckon he'll figure Ringold is behind it. Which in a roundabout sort of way, I guess he is. He'll figure we were workin' for Ringold and will head for the Wine Glass R.'

'So if we're to have any chance of stoppin' Ollinger, our best plan is to do what he expects and head there too?'

'That's the way I see it,' Forrest said. 'And there's another reason why Ollinger will make for the Wine Glass. Accordin' to Cushman, him and Ollinger used to ride together. Seems like they were pretty close till they fell out. He even suspected that Ringold was responsible for takin' the icon in the first place. That gives Ollinger another incentive.' He turned to Dowd, who had said very little. 'What do you think, Father?' he asked.

Father Dowd glanced at Ignacio who had returned and was sitting a little apart. 'Ignacio has found what he was looking for,' he replied. 'He has his icon safe in his keeping. It would make sense for us both to ride on back to Caldera.'

'No,' Forrest said. 'Ignacio wants to be sure that his icon remains safe, but it won't be so long as Ollinger thinks there is treasure to be found and the icons hold the key.'

'Of course you are right,' Father Dowd said. 'But that is not the real reason we will carry on riding with you to the Wine Glass R. Oh yes, we will return to Mexico just as soon as we can, but I know Ignacio and can speak for him as well as myself. I've seen what happened at Mud Wagon Creek and Ignacio has seen enough to know how these bandits operate. They won't stop till somebody stands up to them and we've got no choice but to make the attempt.'

It was Burden's turn to grin. 'Well spoken,' he said. 'I got to admit I didn't twig to what you were sayin' about the mountain business, but I sure cotton to that.'

The fire was sinking low. Out in the night a coyote howled.

'Better get some sleep,' Forrest said. 'We got some hard travellin' tomorrow.'

Forrest was back on familiar ground when he crossed the boundary to Wine Glass range. He had spent some time working for Ringold and it was Ringold who had sent him off to Mexico in quest of the icon of the Virgin of the Sign. He expected to come across indications of activity but the range seemed strangely quiet. They saw nothing of either men or cattle. Only when they rode into the ranch house yard did they come upon one of the ranch-hands, a man Forrest knew only as Slim. He took a few moments to remember Forrest.

'Hell,' he said, 'you been all the way down to Mexico and back and I never even figured you were gone.'

'Where is everybody?' Forrest said.

'Most of the boys have gone off with the cattle.'

'You mean they've started the drive already? Kinda early isn't it?'

The man shrugged. 'The boss seemed to reckon there was no point in waitin' any longer.'

'Is he leadin' the drive?'

'Nope. He's right inside there.' The man jerked his thumb in the direction of the ranch house. Forrest swung down from leather, followed by the others.

'Reckon you can take care of the horses? I got some pretty urgent business with Ringold.'

While Slim took charge of their mounts, they made their way to the ranch house. Before they reached it the door swung open and another man appeared on the porch.

'Forrest, you son of a gun,' he said. 'I'd about given up on seein' you again. What took you so long?'

'Kinda got tangled up,' Forrest replied.

Ringold glanced at Burden, Dowd

and Ignacio. 'These friends of yours?' he said.

'Yeah. Good friends.'

He looked closely at Dowd. 'You look kinda familiar,' he said. 'Have I seen you someplace before?'

'It's all part of why I took so long to get back,' Forrest intervened. 'I need to talk to you, Mr Ringold.'

Ringold nodded. 'Yeah, and I'd be plumb interested in hearin' what you got to say. Why don't you all step on in?'

He led the way and when they were all seated and the introductions had been made, he produced a bottle of good whiskey and poured drinks all round. 'Well,' he said, addressing Dowd, 'Fancy meetin' up with you again. How many years is it? A lot of water must have passed under the bridge between then and now.'

'We were young and foolhardy. Ain't proud of some of the things I got up to then,' Dowd answered.

'Me neither,' Ringold said. 'You got it

right. It don't do no good to go back over those things.'

Forrest took Ringold's comments as his cue. 'Sometimes the past comes right back to kick you,' he said. Ringold gave him a puzzled glance. 'Guess you ain't forgotten Oregon Boot Bass Ollinger,' Forrest added.

Suddenly Ringold was attentive. 'Oregon Boot Bass!' he muttered. 'Last I heard of him he was doin' time in the Oregon State Penitentiary.'

'That was some time ago. He now owns a spread called the Grand Springs.'

'Is that so? Well, I ain't surprised. I've heard rumours that the Grand Springs has been threatenin' to take over some of the other ranches around these parts. Oregon Boot Bass. There was always somethin' about him I didn't like. People like me and Dowd might have been wild, but he was plumb crazy.' He had addressed his last remark to Dowd. Now he turned back to Forrest. 'But what's all this got to do with your trip down Mexico way? Hell, you ain't even said how you met up with this old ridin' partner of mine.'

Forrest took a long swig of the whiskey. 'Guess I'd better start right there,' he said.

'Did you find out about that icon?'

'Like I say, I'd better start at the point you sent me down to Mexico.'

Trying to keep the account as brief as possible, Forrest told his story. There were frequent interruptions from Ringold but when Forrest had finished his main reaction was one of disappointment. 'You say those words written on the back of the icons don't mean nothin',' he said.

'Not exactly nothin',' Dowd replied. 'They just don't have anything to do with any hoard of treasure.'

'The main point,' Forrest said, 'is that Ollinger and his gang could be headed this way right now. We need to do somethin' to prepare ourselves.'

'From what we've seen of him already,' Burden interjected, 'he's gonna stop at nothin' if he thinks those icons

173

will give him the information he wants. And that don't take into account the fact that he's got a personal score to settle with the four of us.'

'He ain't gonna be feelin' right friendly towards me either,' Ringold replied.

'So we got to act, and quick,' Forrest said. He turned to Ringold. 'It's a pity most of your boys are away on a cattle drive.'

'I figured to start early,' Ringold replied. 'Seems like I made a mistake.'

'You weren't to know,' Forrest said.

'They can't have got too far. Maybe I could send for some of 'em to come back?'

'Ollinger could be here any time. We'll have to do the best we can with what we've got.'

Ringold put his glass down on a table and got to his feet. 'Wait a minute,' he said. 'I'll find Slim and get him to see about roundin' up some of the boys out on the range.'

He went out and while he was gone the others continued to drink in silence.

174

It wasn't long before he was back. 'Slim's on his way,' he said. 'More whiskey, gentlemen?'

Back in Mud Wagon Creek the burials had all taken place and the town's reconstruction was making good progress. The school house had just reopened and Miss Louisa Dolan had spent the afternoon reading with the class. At first the children had seemed nervous and unsettled but she soon succeeded in focusing their attention on the story. Her voice was soothing as well as authoritative and she knew how to bring the tale they were reading to life. The nervousness which the children exhibited was a reflection of the mood of the town in general. Despite the improving situation, Miss Dolan sensed an atmosphere of trepidation hanging over the place. The feelings of anger and determination which had accompanied the townsfolk's grief and sorrow had begun to fade, to be replaced by a growing fear that the outlaws might return. Miss Dolan felt something of it herself, but in her case the fear was more personal. She had no way of knowing what had happened to Forrest, Dowd and the marshal since they had ridden out in search of the perpetrators of the atrocity. The lesson had finished and as she sat in an empty classroom at the end of the afternoon she was surprised to find herself thinking of Forrest in particular. It was the first time a man had occupied her thoughts since she had become a widow and she felt a slight pang of guilt. But why should that be the case? He had told her that he had been working for an outfit called the Wine Glass R and that he and his companion were merely passing through. Yet he had stayed to help out and then undertaken the dangerous task of bringing the outlaws to justice. What were his chances, the chances of the three of them, against an entire band of ruthless desperados? Would she ever see him again? Then she was struck by another odd thought. Without the dreadful events that had occurred, she would never have met him.

Marshal Kip Arnold and the posse had run into some difficulties following the trail of the outlaws from Stinkweed, but when he found the bodies by the river he knew he was on the right track. There was little doubt in his mind that they were the remains of some of the owlhoots who had carried out the bank robbery and held up the stage, but who had shot them? There was evidence that a lot more of the gunnies had been involved so whoever had been in the fight had put up a good show.

'What do you make of it?' one of the men asked.

'I don't know, but it looks like those gun-totin' varmints made some more enemies.'

'You sure these are some of 'em? Could be more of their victims.'

'Reckon I can recognize an owlhoot dead or alive,' the marshal replied. He looked more closely at the surrounding area. 'My opinion is that someone apart from us is trailin' these varmints and the outlaws probably know it. My guess is that a group of 'em were assigned to deal with it but they didn't do a very good job.'

'If that's the case, I'll sure look forward with meetin' 'em.'

Arnold climbed back into leather. 'Me too,' he said. 'Let's just hope we meet up with 'em before the outlaws do. Those varmints are gonna be more mad than ever when they know about what's happened here.'

6

Forrest, Ringold and Burden had, among them, worked out a plan of campaign. At first their intention had been to fortify the ranch house at the Wine Glass R and meet Ollinger there. Burden, however, had pointed out the disadvantages of getting pinned down.

'We'd have plenty of cover, but what if they decided to play a waitin' game? They could take their time and just wait till we run out of supplies.'

'Not much fear of that,' Ringold said. 'We got plenty and there's a well right in the cellar.'

'I don't reckon Ollinger would be that patient,' Forrest said.

'OK, but he might try to burn us out.'

'That's more likely,' Forrest said. 'I don't figure it would take a lot to set this place ablaze.'

They considered the matter and then Forrest came up with an idea. 'Ollinger may not expect much opposition. After all, he's no way of knowing we're here. He'll probably realize that a lot of the ranch-hands are away.'

'In that case, he'll certainly hope to find Ringold at home,' Burden interjected.

'Yes. So why don't we do something he won't be expectin' and leave the ranch unattended.'

'The place would be at his mercy,' Ringold objected.

'That's just the point,' Forrest answered. 'In one sense you're right, but on the other hand, if we do that, it'll be Ollinger and his gang bottled up in here and not us.'

'I hope you ain't proposin' to set fire to the ranch house,' Ringold said.

Forrest looked at him hard. 'If it comes to it,' he replied. For a moment Ringold thought he was joking but the grim set of Forrest's jaw soon disabused him.

'It's either us or him and he'll have by far the advantage in numbers,' Forrest said. 'Believe me, it's gonna take whatever we need to do.'

'I can remember Ollinger,' Ringold replied after a moment's reflection, 'and I guess you're right.'

'So, we'll let Ollinger ride in and then we'll attack,' Burden interjected.

'No,' Forrest said. 'We let him and his men settle in and make themselves comfortable. Then, when they least expect it, we attack.'

Burden considered the proposition. 'We could try and pick him off as he rides in,' he said.

'I've thought about it,' Forrest said. 'It would be a good plan if we had more men, but there are just not enough of us.'

'I think Forrest is right,' Father Dowd put in. Forrest looked at the others for confirmation.

'OK, agreed,' Ringold said, 'but how about we place men in the barn and stables?'

Forrest took another moment to consider the suggestion. 'I think it might be better if we just give the whole place over to Ollinger and stay in the open,' he replied.

'I sure don't like the idea of that varmint takin' charge of my ranch,' Ringold said, 'but like you say, I guess it's what we're gonna have to do.'

'I'm afraid the ranch is goin' to take a beating whatever happens,' Forrest said.

Once the decision was made, the details were relatively easy. Ringold positioned his men at strategic points around the ranch with Burden and Slim while he, Forrest, Ignacio and Dowd placed themselves behind some rocks on a hill just behind the ranch house. Before they took up their stations they checked their weapons and made sure they had plenty of ammunition. When they had finished Forrest looked at his little bunch of fighters. They seemed a worryingly small number.

'Hell,' he said, 'I was goin' to say I hope we're right about Ollinger showin' up, but now I ain't so sure.'

'We ain't scared,' Slim said.

'Sure appreciate your attitude,' Ringold replied.

'We been ridin' for you a long time, Mr Ringold. We owe it to the brand.'

'We got the icons,' Ignacio said. 'They give us power Ollinger can't deal with.'

'I hope you're right,' Forrest replied. 'When we started after Ollinger, there were two of us. Then two became four. Now we're ten.'

'Twelve if Ignacio's right and you count the icons,' Father Dowd said.

Forrest grinned. 'Yeah. That means the odds have increased by six times in our favour. We got more than enough. Let's get to it.'

The hours slipped by. Forrest was convinced that Ollinger would appear but he didn't know when. From time to time he glanced across at Ringold, who was the nearest to him. It was odd to think that Ringold and Father Dowd had once ridden the owlhoot trail alongside the man they were waiting for. Ringold acknowledged Forrest's look by raising his rifle. Forrest was tempted to get out his tobacco pouch and roll himself a cigarette but he didn't want to take any chance of being detected, no matter how small. He looked over the top of the boulder he was sheltering behind to the ranch house below. The place looked what for the moment it was — deserted. Would the very shortage of people and activity alert the outlaws? Like Forrest, they would probably notice how quiet it was on the range and put it down to Ringold's men having started on a trail drive. Rather than alerting them, it might make them more careless. His gaze wandered to the other buildings and the empty corrals beyond. Although the cattle had gone, their smell still pervaded the air. He shuffled about and changed positions. Then he saw the dust cloud which could only presage the arrival of Ollinger and his gunslicks. Ringold had seen it too. Getting to his feet, Forrest gave the signal to warn the others, although he had no doubt that they would already have noticed it.

The dark clouds grew and spread and then through the haze of dust Ollinger and his outlaw gang began to materialize. Forrest had brought his field glasses along with him and now he put them to his eyes. With their aid he could count upward of thirty riders. They were coming on in a wide arc, riding at a steady trot, and the sound of their horses' hoofs as they got closer was thunderous. When they got near they began to bunch up and as they rode into the yard the dust was so thick that Forrest could hardly see them. The dust soon lifted to reveal the riders gathered together. It was obvious that they were a little puzzled at the absence of people; they had probably been expecting some sort of reaction to their arrival. One of them swung down from his horse and, although he had never met him before, Forrest could tell by the way he limped that it must be Oregon Boot Bass himself. For a moment

185

he stood with his hands on his hips, looking all about him. The voices of some of his men rose to Forrest's ears and there was a continuous stamping and snorting of horses. Some of the other riders began to dismount. One of them came forward and exchanged words with Ollinger and then Ollinger turned and hobbled up the porch steps. He paused for a moment, looking back at his men, before rapping loudly on the door. When nothing happened he knocked again and then waved impatiently for the second man to come forward. Again they exchanged words and then the man lifted his foot and brought it crashing into the door. Another man stepped up and they repeated the process. After a few moments the door began to splinter and then what was left of it swung open. Drawing their guns, Ollinger and his henchmen stepped inside. After a few moments they emerged and Ollinger shouted to the rest of his men.

'There's nobody here! Make yourselves at home, boys!'

His words were greeted by an immediate outburst of shouts, whoops and gunshots as the outlaws dropped from their saddles and made their way into the ranch house to celebrate. Presently a number of them re-emerged with bottles held to their mouths; a few began to round up the horses and lead them in the direction of the stables. Forrest was glad that he had taken the decision not to place men in any of the buildings. The risk of discovery would have been too great. The noise from inside the ranch house was loud and raucous; there was a fresh outburst of gunfire and some of the windows shattered. Ringold started to move but Forrest waved him back. Ringold's features were grim. Forrest realized how hard it must be for Ringold to see what the outlaws were doing to his house, but it was important not to give the game away. The outlaws had already raided Ringold's stock of liquor; give them some time, Forrest thought, and they might have drunk themselves into a state of stupefaction before night fell. Forrest glanced up the hillside but his men were well concealed. It was a question now of holding their nerve. He was just about to alter his position ready for a long wait when suddenly he heard a shout from one of the men in the yard. At the same moment the man raised his rifle and fired. The report rang out and was answered by a crack from somewhere behind the barn. The men in the yard started to run as the remaining horses reared and began to scatter.

'Hell!' Forrest exclaimed out loud. 'That's done it!'

He could only assume that one of Ringold's men had revealed his position. The gunnies in the yard had dispersed, most of them taking shelter in the ranch house from which a barrage of fire was now booming, to be answered by a fusillade of shots from the surrounding brush. Realizing that his carefully made plans were now useless, Forrest shouted to his men on the hillside.

'Commence fire!'

Immediately, a furious cannonade resounded behind and above him, echoing from the rocks. Ringold was already blasting away and Forrest followed suit, pumping lead at the ranch house. Stabs of flame were issuing from the windows and smoke was billowing across the yard. Smoke and flame were coming from both the stables and the barn; some of Ollinger's men had obviously sought shelter within. Forrest didn't mind that so much, but what did concern him were the sounds of shots coming from points around the ranch house where neither he nor Ringold had posted anybody. It could only mean that not all the outlaws were pinned inside the building. Most of the outlaws' horses had stampeded but a few were still lingering around the sides of the building and a few of them lay in the yard where they had been felled. He was concentrating his fire on the front of the ranch house and so was taken by surprise when, from the back, a bunch of Ollinger's men suddenly burst clear, making a dash for cover behind the empty corrals. He raised his sights and began to fire at them but the rush had caught him by surprise. Shots were coming from some of Ringold's men and Forrest saw at least two of the gunnies go down, but most of them made it to safety. Now their position had really deteriorated. Not only had they lost the initiative and failed to keep the gunnies cooped up, but Ollinger had a good idea of their dispositions and substantial numbers of his men were in a position to try and circumvent them. His brain was racing, trying to calculate a response. Taking advantage of a slight lull in the shooting, he glanced over at Ringold. To his horror the rancher was stretched out on the ground. Breaking cover, Forrest began to slither forwards. Bullets were clipping the rocks uncomfortably close and the whine of their ricochets sang in his ears. Coming alongside Ringold, he was relieved to see that the rancher was still breathing.

'Have you been hit?' he breathed.

'It's my thigh,' Ringold replied. 'It must have ricocheted off a rock.'

Forrest looked down. A red stain was spreading across Ringold's trousers. Quickly, Forrest took his knife and cut through the material. The bullet seemed to have seared through the fleshy part of Ringold's leg; it was bleeding quite badly but it did not appear to be really serious. Forrest's main concern was the continuing loss of blood. Taking off his bandanna, he fastened it as tightly as he could around the leg above the wound. Then he unfastened Ringold's bandanna and pressed it hard to staunch the blood.

'Hold it as tight as you can,' he said. At that moment a volley of shots went pinging around the rocks behind which they were sheltered.

'I'll be OK,' Ringold said. 'You'd better get back to the action.'

'Do you reckon you could move with my help?' Forrest said.

'I could give it a try,' Ringold replied,

'but it might be better to leave me.'

Ignoring Ringold's last comment, Forrest began helping him to his knees. 'Follow me if you can,' he said.

'Why? Where are we goin'?'

'This position is becoming impossible,' Forrest replied. 'I want to get up the hill to the others and make a retreat.'

Ringold grimaced. 'I hope you ain't thinkin' of lettin' Ollinger get away with anythin'.'

'One thing at a time,' Forrest replied. 'I'm not likely to forget that coyote.'

Forrest began to crawl away and Ringold followed, wincing with pain. Hearing a gasp, Forrest looked back but Ringold waved him on. It was slow going and all the time bullets were whizzing overhead or exploding against the rocks, sending up slivers of metal and granite. Although they were making a strenuous effort, it seemed to Forrest that they weren't making much progress. From time to time he glanced behind him and uttered a few words of encouragement, but Ringold's sighs and groans were enough to assure him that the rancher was still there. When it seemed they would never make it to higher ground, Forrest heard the scuffle of boots. He swung his rifle to a shooting position and then heaved a sigh of relief when he saw that it was not one of Ollinger's gunnies, but Dowd.

'What's happening?' Dowd said.

'Ringold's been hit.'

One glance at Ringold was enough to apprise Dowd of the situation. 'Here, let me give you a hand,' he said.

He climbed down so that he was below the level of Ringold and then between them he and Forrest succeeded in assisting the injured man to the safety of the bushes where Ignacio had remained in concealment. Ringold lay gasping, sweat gathered on his brow and running down his cheeks. Below them the rattle of gunfire continued unabated. Dowd bent down to attend to the injured man and Ignacio turned to Forrest.

'Things have not gone according to plan,' he said.

'I'm not sure what happened,' Forrest replied. 'I think one of the gunslicks must have spotted one of our men.'

'What can we do?' Ignacio said.

'Right now I think we need to retreat and regroup. I'm hopin' Burden thinks the same, but we need to get a message to the others.'

He turned to Ringold. 'You sure you're OK for the time bein'?' he said.

'Sure. Just leave me here and do whatever needs to be done.'

Forrest nodded. 'Right. Then this is what I propose. Me and Ignacio will make our way to the others as best we can, goin' in separate directions. When we've made contact we'll all move back. Meetin' here would be as good as anywhere. Once we've done that we can decide together on what the next move should be.'

'What about me?' Dowd said.

'Someone had better stay with Ringold. You're more use in this sort of situation than me or Ignacio.'

Hearing Forrest's words, Ringold

194

struggled to sit upright. 'Like I said, I'll be OK,' he muttered. 'You can't afford to leave Dowd sittin' up here.' Forrest wasn't sure. He looked at Dowd.

'I've dressed the wound,' Dowd said. 'The bleeding has more or less stopped. He'll be OK for now. At some point later we'll need to get the bullet out.'

'All right,' Forrest said. 'You go with Ignacio. Now let's get movin'.'

Dowd and Ignacio set off in one direction while Forrest took another. Going down the hill was comparatively easy without Ringold and there were fewer bullets exploding all around. Forrest's difficulties began as he reached the bottom. There was less cover and if he was spotted he would have to run a gauntlet of gunfire. Shots were coming from all directions and he was running the additional risk of being fired on from his own side. He was at the back of the house and he needed to skirt round it. Concentrating on what he was doing, he barely noticed a loose horse coming up behind him. At the same moment a shot rang out and the horse let out a loud whinny of pain. Forrest spun round to see a man with a smoking rifle. As the horse plunged by he squeezed the trigger of his own Winchester and the man went spinning backwards. Forrest fired once more and the man slumped to the floor. Forrest realized how lucky he had been; the man was close and the horse had taken the shot which had been meant for him. Realizing that some of the other gunnies had probably seen him, he took to his heels and ran fast. Shots began to ring out from behind him, tearing up dust. Ahead of him three gunnies appeared and he swerved as their guns spat lead. Another shot rang out and, as one of the gunnies fell, Burden stepped out from the shelter of some bushes, firing rapidly. One of the remaining gunnies collapsed while the other started to run, dodging and weaving as he went. Burden let him go, turning to Forrest. 'This way,' he said.

They both plunged into the cover of the bushes. More shots were booming at their rear and they kept running till they felt sure they had shaken off any pursuers, at least for the time being. They fell to the floor, both panting.

'I didn't expect to see you,' Burden said.

'You sure appeared at the right moment,' Forrest replied.

Burden peered from their shelter, checking that no one was near them. The crash of gunfire was muted and had grown more sporadic.

'Things aren't lookin' good,' Forrest said. 'Ringold's been wounded. I figured to get down here and spread the message to retreat.'

'Sounds sensible, but it's a bit late as far as the men I was with are concerned. There's only one of 'em left standin'. I told him to get out of it while he still can. I don't know how it is with Slim and the rest.'

'Dowd and Ignacio are lookin' for 'em. We arranged to meet up at the top of the hill.'

'Not the best idea. We might get

197

trapped up there.'

'I had no choice. I had to leave Ringold.'

'OK. Then I suggest we start makin' it back.'

As they made their way through the scrub they became conscious that the rattle of gunfire had ceased. Instead they could hear the muffled sounds of voices shouting.

'Looks like Ollinger and his boys are celebrating,' Burden said, 'but it won't be long till they start huntin' for the rest of us.'

Forrest had become disoriented and for a time he couldn't find the spot where he had left Ringold. In the end it was the rancher's groans which brought them to where he was lying. With him were Ignacio and Dowd and two of Ringold's ranch-hands, including Slim.

'We were wonderin' where you'd got to,' Slim said.

'How is Ringold?' Forrest asked Dowd.

'Not so good. I've done the best I

can, but he's goin' to need help soon.'

Just as Forrest was about to reply, there came a loud outburst of shooting from the bottom of the hill. People were shouting and whooping. Forrest moved away and glanced down. The gunslicks were congregating in the yard at the front of the ranch house and some of them were looking towards the hill.

'Looks to me like Ollinger and his boys are on their way,' he said. He glanced down at Ringold and added, 'we're gonna have to carry him.' He bent down and explained what was happening. Ringold managed to raise the shadow of a smile.

'Don't worry 'bout me,' he said. 'Do what you have to.'

Forrest stood up. 'Help get him on my back,' he said.

With the assistance of Dowd and Ignacio, the injured rancher was lifted up so that Forrest could carry him. The sounds of gunfire were louder and they could see the outlaws moving away from the ranch house. They began to walk. There was a slight climb to the top of the hill, beyond which it ran level before dropping to form a grassy shelf. The first part was heavy going for Forrest with the weight of the rancher bearing him down. At the same time, he was trying to step as carefully as he could so as not to cause Ringold more suffering than he could help. When they had almost reached the crest of the hill, he paused to glance back. The outlaws were spreading out all around and a group of them had started climbing the hill. They seemed not to have seen any of them yet but it could be only a matter of time till they did. Even as they prepared to move on, a fresh volume of shouting burst out and gunshots began to crackle.

'I think they've seen us,' Burden commented. They started forward but after a few paces Forrest stopped them.

'It's no use,' he said. 'We'll never make it.'

'Leave me,' Ringold muttered. 'I'm slowin' you down too much.'

'That ain't got nothin' to do with it,' Forrest said. 'We should have thought of this and left our horses somewhere we could get to 'em.'

'We weren't to know,' Burden said.

'We ain't gonna get far so the only option we got left is to make a stand of it here on top of the hill. At least we got some cover.'

Nobody argued the point so they quickly set about making themselves as inconspicuous as possible. Shots were striking the rocks close to them now; although they could not see anything as yet of their attackers, they began to return fire. Smoke was rising from the bushes below, indicating where the gunnies were advancing.

'Hold fire!' Forrest shouted.

The others did as he commanded. Presently the gunnies in the forefront of the attack began to appear.

'Fire!' Forrest screamed. His rifle kicked as he squeezed the trigger. Burden had run out of ammunition and was using his six-guns. Ignacio and Dowd were both blasting away and the gunslicks' bullets were ripping up the hillside all around them. Forrest felt a bullet tug at the sleeve of his jacket but he carried on, firing now with his six-guns like Burden. The combined onslaught seemed to halt the outlaws in their tracks because there was a lull in the firing. Forrest jammed more slugs into his guns and glanced across at the others. They were making a good fight but he knew it was hopeless. There were just too many of the gunslicks. His original plan might have stood a chance of working, but it was no use thinking about that now. He wondered if the others realized how desperate their situation was when his ears picked up the sound of horses somewhere beyond the brow of the hill. His stomach sank. If the outlaws had ridden round and outflanked them, they had even less chance of survival. The sound of the horses grew louder and it was accompanied by the sound of gunfire. Forrest looked at Burden. 'Come with me!' he shouted. 'We'll try and hold 'em off.'

Crouched low, they scrambled to the top of the hill. Their ears had not deceived them. A substantial number of horsemen had appeared. Some of them were circling near the ranch house which they could just see around the curve of the hill, but others were riding up the long slope towards the ledge which lay beyond where they were lying. Burden had reloaded his rifle and was about to take aim at one of the riders when Forrest called out to him.

'Hold it! There's somethin' odd goin' on. If those riders are Ollinger's boys, they sure seem to be actin' strangely.'

For a few moments they watched the struggle below. Some of the riders had galloped straight into the yard of the ranch and others had dismounted and taken cover. They were firing in the direction of the ranch house. The ones coming up the slope began to open fire but they were not aiming in the direction of Forrest and Burden. Forrest strained his eyes, trying to make out what was happening. When the riders reached the flat grassy bench they dismounted and continued on foot. The man at the forefront was big and something gleamed on his chest. Suddenly Forrest realized it was a marshal's badge.

'Hell!' he shouted, 'They ain't Ollinger's boys. It's the law.'

The men came on and Forrest realized they needed to make the newcomers aware of their position and that they had nothing to do with Ollinger.

'Hello!' he yelled. 'Don't shoot. We're on the same side.'

The noise of gunfire was getting louder and none of the new arrivals seemed to hear him. He tried once more but it was obvious he needed to do something more drastic. Ripping part of his white shirt, he sprang to his feet and began to wave it in the air. A bullet passed uncomfortably close but then the newcomers stopped and the leader held out his arm,

'Get up and show them your badge!'

Forrest called to Burden.

In a moment Burden was on his feet, exposing the tin star on his jacket. Forrest's heart was in his mouth. Had they understood? At any moment one of them might take it into his head to shoot at them. He exchanged glances with Burden and then they both stepped forward. The leader suddenly ran forward and in a few moments they were exchanging handshakes.

'The name's Arnold,' the big man said.

'My name's Forrest and this is Burden, Marshal of Mud Wagon Creek.'

Arnold looked closely at him. 'I've heard your name,' he said. He turned back to Forrest. 'Where's Ollinger?' he snapped.

'A lot of his men are on the other side of the hill. You got here just in time.'

There were four others in addition to Arnold. Together with Forrest and Burden, they ran to the crest of the hill and dropped over the other side to where Dowd and Ignacio were continuing to hold back the outlaws.

'Time we went on the offensive,' Forrest said. He and Burden exchanged a few words with Arnold. 'We'll spread out and start takin' the battle to Ollinger.'

They quickly put the plan into effect, feeling confident that now their numbers were increased and with more of Arnold's posse tackling the outlaws around the ranch, the odds had swung in their favour. Ollinger might still have a lot more men, but they would be badly discouraged by the injection of fresh forces against them. As they advanced they spread a heavy hail of lead in front of them and Forrest soon had the feeling that the outlaws were beginning to wilt. The answering fire began to dwindle and soon he was coming across bodies lying in the undergrowth. When he looked towards the ranch he seemed to detect a similar story, and his view of things was confirmed when a bunch of riders suddenly appeared at the back of the ranch house, riding hard away from the scene of the struggle. It could only be some of Ollinger's gunnies making good their escape. A new question disturbed Forrest's mind: was Ollinger amongst them? He looked left and right. Dowd, Burden and Ignacio were moving forwards in line with him and a little way beyond he could make out Arnold and some of the posse. They were meeting with little opposition now and when they reached the bottom of the hill it was clear that the gunnies had given up the battle. Two of them rode past on stray horses they had succeeded in getting hold of but they were too intent on getting away to even fire. One of them turned and shouted: 'Rawlins! Watch out!' A third horseman appeared round the corner of the barn with his gun ready. He turned his horse and began to ride away from Forrest at the same moment that Ignacio emerged from cover. The man raised his six-gun and fired at Ignacio who staggered back a step and then fell, clutching his chest. Steadying himself, Forrest squeezed the trigger of his revolver. As the smoke cleared, for a few moments it looked like the man had got away but then he swayed and came tumbling out of the saddle. He got to his feet but before he could return fire another bullet from Forrest's gun smashed into him and Rawlins toppled dead as a felled log.

Forgetting the man, Forrest rushed to Ignacio, who lay prone on the ground. Forrest feared the worst. He bent down and gathered his stricken comrade in his arms. A trickle of blood was issuing from Ignacio's mouth but otherwise Forrest could see no sign of injury. Suddenly, to his surprise, Ignacio's eyes opened and a faint smile spread across his lined features.

'I told you the icon was on our side,' he said. 'I knew the Virgin of the Sign would keep me safe.'

Forrest was uncomprehending. 'What do you mean?' he said. 'Have you been wounded?'

Ignacio shook his head. 'My chest hurts but nothing more.'

'Must have been when you fell.'

'No, it is nothing like that. The man shot me but I had the icon in my pocket.'

Forrest looked more closely. Ignacio's shirt was torn and there was a livid mark where a bullet had seared its way across his flesh.

'The bullet glanced off the icon,' Ignacio said. 'The Virgin saved me.'

He sat up and, feeling in his pocket, withdrew the icon. There was a burn mark on the wrappings but when he peered inside the icon had received no worse damage than a dent in one corner. 'It is a miracle,' he said.

Forrest wasn't sure whether he was referring to his own survival or that of the icon, but it certainly seemed that Ignacio had been very lucky. There was no doubt in his mind that if the bullet hadn't deflected, Ignacio would be dead.

When Ignacio had succeeded in struggling to his feet, the pair of them set off in the direction of the ranch. Shooting was still taking place but it was apparent that Arnold's men had succeeded in gaining the upper hand even before the arrival of their leader. The few outlaws who remained were in process of being rounded up under the supervision of Arnold and Burden. Forrest and Ignacio met with Dowd on the ranch house porch.

'I wonder what's become of Ollinger?' Dowd said.

'I don't know, but I bet when we go inside he'll have turned the place upside down huntin' for that icon.'

'Let's take a look,' Dowd said.

Forrest wasn't wrong, but the damage that had been caused to the ranch house was due to more than Ollinger's search for the icon. The outlaws had let rip and the place was a shambles. Ringold's collection of paintings had been torn from the walls and most of his pottery and ceramics lay smashed on the floor.

'Ringold's goin' to have quite a job on his hands getting this place back to normal,' Dowd commented. His words reminded them that Ringold was still lying injured at the top of the hill.

'I'll get back there right now,' Forrest said. 'You two see if you can find some medicines and then round up a couple of Arnold's men and come up after me.'

Quickly, he turned on his heels and left the room. If the scene inside the house was one of desolation, the outside prospect was only marginally better. For the first time Forrest observed how shot-up and damaged the ranch house was. He didn't take any time to dwell on it, but made his way quickly towards the hill. Compared with before, the walk up the hill was easy, but he was still breathless as he approached the spot where they had left Ringold. The place was now oddly peaceful after what had gone before and he was off his guard as he approached the patch of brush where Ringold was concealed. He was taken completely by surprise when a man stepped out from behind a rock with a rifle in his hands. As the man limped forward, Forrest knew it was Ollinger.

'Me and Mr Ringold have just been

renewin' acquaintances,' he said.

Forrest was suddenly alarmed, not for his own safety, but for Ringold's. 'You dirty skunk,' he said. 'You better not have hurt him.'

An evil leer spread itself across the outlaw's countenance. 'Don't worry. Ringold is safe. For the moment. In view of circumstances, I think it's yourself you need to be concerned about.'

'How did you get up here?' Forrest said.

'Oh, I didn't come up the hard way. I rode up, same as that scum from the posse did. And I'll be ridin' away just as soon as I've dealt with you.' He levered the rifle and pointed it at Forrest. 'I figure you're the varmint broke into my ranch house recently. In fact, one way and another, I reckon you been causin' me a heap of trouble.'

'That what Cushman told you?' Forrest said.

Ollinger let out an ugly laugh. 'Cushman? He was a fool. Now, you got one chance to live.'

'Yeah? What's that?' Forrester said.

'Since we both know what you took from that safe, you'd better tell me where that treasure is.'

Forrest looked blank.

'You didn't take that thing for nothin'. So I'll ask just once more: where's the treasure?'

'I don't know what you're talkin' about,' Forrest said.

Suddenly the look on Ollinger's face darkened. Stepping forward, he slammed the muzzle of the rifle into Forrest's belly, swinging it up immediately into his face. Forrest doubled up and then staggered back, blood pouring from a deep gash which had opened up his chin. Blood jetted out like a fountain. Ollinger stood over him and jammed the gun into his temple.

'You'd better start talkin' and quick,' he said.

Pain seared through Forrest's stomach and jaw. He felt sick and his head was swimming.

'Don't keep me waitin',' Ollinger hissed.

Forrest opened his mouth but he couldn't speak. His vision had tightened to a concentrated focus on Ollinger's hand. He saw Ollinger's finger begin to close on the trigger of the rifle and through a gathering darkness he heard a shattering explosion. In a suspension of time he knew it was the end. But then he opened his eyes and, somehow, time had resumed. He couldn't understand how or why he was still there and then a face formed itself out of the air and looked down on him.

'Forrest! Forrest! Are you hurt bad?'

The face was blurred and vague and then it began to assume features till he was able to recognize it. 'Ringold!' he gasped.

He tried to raise himself but fell back. Then Ringold, ignoring the pain in his leg, had his arms round his shoulders and was lending him his support. With his assistance he managed to sit up and then he was sick. When he had stopped retching he looked up into Ringold's face.

'Hell, we're a pair,' he said.

For the first time he became aware of Ollinger's body lying in the grass nearby and the gun which Ringold still held.

'I thought Ollinger's rifle might have gone off too,' Ringold said, 'but there was nothin' else I could do.' He glanced at the six-gun in his hand. 'I had to make it count,' he said. 'It was my last bullet.'

Suddenly they heard the stamp of boots. Ringold looked round in alarm but it was only Dowd and Ignacio. Just behind them were a couple of members of Arnold's posse. Forrest managed a grim smile.

'Hope you found those medicines,' he said. 'We're both gonna need whatever you got.'

★ ★ ★

It was late at night before a semblance of normality was restored to the Wine Glass R. Some of the obvious damage

215

to the ranch house had been repaired and things set more or less straight. Some of the paintings were restored to the walls but most of Ringold's other things were damaged beyond repair. Ringold lay on a sofa. The bullet had been removed from the fleshy part of his leg by Dowd and although the wound was bad and he had lost a lot of blood, it was not as serious as they had at first thought. Forrest's chin was slashed to the bone and his stomach was sore, but he had come through a lot worse.

'At least there's one good thing about those varmints catchin' sight of us,' Burden said as he raised a glass of whiskey to his lips.

'Yeah? What's that?' Forrest replied.

'They didn't have time to finish off Ringold's stock of liquor.'

Forrest started to laugh but then doubled up in a paroxysm of pain.

'You're goin' to have quite a bruise,' Arnold said.

Ringold turned to Dowd. 'You sure done a good job fixin' that leg,' he said.

'You ever trained as a doctor?'

'No. I just kinda picked it up,' he replied.

'Well, I appreciate what you done for me. In fact, I appreciate what you all done for me. As far as the damage goes, I guess most things are replaceable. Without you happenin' along, I reckon there wouldn't be anythin' left of me or the Wine Glass R.'

'That varmint Ollinger and his gang deserved everythin' they got,' Arnold remarked. 'It's goin' to take a long time before either Burden's town or mine recover from what they did.'

They lapsed into temporary silence while they savoured Ringold's best whiskey. Arnold's remark served to remind Forrest of Mud Wagon Creek and he suddenly felt a longing to see Miss Dolan again.

'I expect you'll be headin' right on back,' he said, addressing Burden and Arnold.

'Yup,' Arnold said. 'I didn't figure to be gone too long and the boys in the

217

posse got their business to attend.'

'Me too,' Burden replied. He looked at Forrest. 'Say, why don't you come back to Mud Wagon Creek? Father Dowd and Ignacio too?'

Forrest turned to Dowd. 'Well?' he said.

Father Dowd shook his head. 'That's real considerate of you, but I reckon me and Ignacio will be heading straight back to Caldera. I've been gone too long already.'

'The Virgin of the Sign will soon be back in her rightful place,' Ignacio said.

Forrest glanced at Dowd. It seemed to him that the erstwhile priest would be back in his rightful place too. He sensed Dowd's conviction that it was there he could best atone for the wrongs he felt he had caused.

Ringold raised himself on his sofa. 'Why don't you take the other icon with you? I can't think of any better place for it. What do you say, boys?' He sank back again as the others voiced their agreement.

'Sure seems the right thing,' Forrest said. 'Those two icons belong together with the people of Caldera.' They raised their glasses and drank and then Burden turned again to Forrest.

'You haven't answered my question,' he said.

'What question was that?' Forrest replied.

'About coming back with me to Mud Wagon Creek.'

Forrest paused for a moment before replying and Miss Dolan's image passed across his mind. 'Yeah,' he said. 'I guess that seems the right thing, too.'

THE END

We do hope that you have enjoyed reading this large print book.

Did you know that all of our titles are available for purchase?

We publish a wide range of high quality large print books including:
Romances, Mysteries, Classics
General Fiction
Non Fiction and Westerns

Special interest titles available in large print are:
The Little Oxford Dictionary
Music Book, Song Book
Hymn Book, Service Book

Also available from us courtesy of Oxford University Press:
Young Readers' Dictionary
(large print edition)
Young Readers' Thesaurus
(large print edition)

For further information or a free brochure, please contact us at:
Ulverscroft Large Print Books Ltd.,
The Green, Bradgate Road, Anstey,
Leicester, LE7 7FU, England.
Tel: (00 44) **0116 236 4325**
Fax: (00 44) **0116 234 0205**

GONE TO BLAZES

Jackson Davis

In the Longhorn saloon in the rambunctious gold rush town of White Oaks, New Mexico, young sawyer Vince falls for the beautiful dancer Selina. But he stands no chance against Texan killer Cotton Bulloch, who kidnaps and brutally forces himself on her. Meanwhile, Jake Blackman and his boys flood the area with forged greenbacks. Can Sheriff Pat Garrett put paid to both Bulloch and Blackman? Must Vince face the murderous Texan alone? And is his love for Selina doomed?

AGAINST ALL ODDS

Hank J. Kirby

Matt Ronan didn't even carry a gun. It wasn't necessary when he was so good with his fists. But after a fatal altercation with a kid, he began to see he was perhaps too good — especially as the boy had a mighty powerful father and brother who would be waiting for Ronan when he was finally released from prison. It seemed like the moment to start packing a gun. He was going to need every advantage he could get . . .

BLOOD TRAIL

Corba Sunman

Greg Bannock raises cattle with his father Pete, until rustlers steal their herd — marking the beginning of bad times for their family. But hiding behind a mask of respectability, there is a renegade at work . . . Assisting deputy sheriff Mack Ketchum, Greg finds himself caught up in a plot to kill the rustler gang boss and has to shoot his way out of trouble, still determined to retrieve his herd. When the gun smoke clears, there is a trail of blood throughout the county.

THE VENOM OF IRON EYES

Rory Black

The notorious gang led by Peg Leg Grimes is headed to the remote and peaceful town of Cooperville to rob the bank of its recently obtained horde of golden eagles. But unknown to the gang, the bounty hunter Iron Eyes is in town to collect a reward. When the bank explodes into matchwood, Iron Eyes vows to get the money, and the outlaws — for Grimes has made one mistake: he has stolen Iron Eyes' prized Palomino stallion to make his escape . . .

MONTAINE'S REVENGE

Dale Graham

Days before the end of the Civil War, Sergeant Cody Montaine is gunned down and left for dead by a bunch of deserters led by Butte Fresno. He survives the vicious attack, but loses his memory. Taking the name of Lucky Johnson, he sets out to piece his life back together. Periodic recollections lead Cody to the town of Las Vegas, where Fresno has assumed his identity. Will Cody get revenge and so exhume his old life?

A TOWN CALLED PERDITION

Lee Lejeune

Jesse 'Mav' Bolder heads into Pure Water, known as Perdition because of its evil reputation. There he encounters some very shady characters, among them the sheriff, Bill Bronco, and local rancher Bunce and his hired killers. But there are good people in Pure Water too and when Mav befriends them, Sheriff Bronco sees it as an opportunity to run them off, leading to a bloody showdown for control of the town.